W9-BZI-115

WILD IS THE WIND

ADVENTURES OF
JEAN PAUL DEBROSSE

RICHARD LOUIS FEDERER

ISBN 978-0-9827101-3-5 Hardback
ISBN 978-0-9827101-0-4 Paperback
Fiction-Action/Adventure/Historical

Cover design:
www.DustinMyersDesign.com 573-308-6060

Special acknowledgement to William G. Federer
for original illustrations on pages 19, 51, 54, 68, 71, 110,
114, 131, 137, 154, 200, 211, 220.

Special thanks to Winnie Carter for her invaluable help as
editor and amenuensis, whose tireless assistance has made
this book a reality.

Amerisearch, Inc., P.O. Box 20163, St. Louis, MO 63123
1-888-USA-WORD, 314-487-4395, 314-487-4489fax
www.amerisearch.net, wjfederer@gmail.com

*To the Love
of
My Life*

Tirzah

❧

TABLE OF
CONTENTS

During France's Reign of Terror, 1793-1794, over 40,000 were beheaded in the guillotine in Paris.

FOREWORD

One of the tragic differences between the American Revolution of 1776 and the French Revolution of 1789 was the disparity of objects of the revolt in each case.

In America, the revolt was against the British Crown, and its governmental behavior towards the American colonies. Britain wanted to retain its lucrative source of income through a punitive taxation system. They did not wish to change the people and culture of the colonies, but rather encourage its commerce so Britain could reap a continuous and ever growing source of wealth.

In France, the revolt was directed against its own people, its own leaders, its own culture, it own religion and even against its own history. Revolutionaries wanted to remake their own people. At first, they would try to do this through reason using the intellectual efforts of Voltaire, Rousseau, and other writers of the philosophs group.

The salons of the highly influential Jacobin and Girondin clubs provided a sounding board for all the radical new ideas that flooded over France.

The edicts of the revolutionary committees of the government confirmed into law even the wildest ideas of their leaders.

Finally, if compliance was tentative, lax, or ignored the revolutionaries had one more card to play; the guillotine.

Engineered, approved, and happily sanctioned as the most efficient way of killing people, the guillotine became the adored symbol and indeed the holy grail of the revolution. Danton, Marat, Robespierre and a host of lesser lights were its high priests. It beheaded between forty and sixty men, women, and children per day for three years.

It was estimated that 40,000 French people paid for this bloody experiment of social change with their lives. King Louis XVI, monarch of France was the first to pay the ultimate price for this futile dash into the maelstrom of death. His wife, Marie Antoinette would soon suffer the same fate. Their daughter Marie Therese Charlotte would escape, but history cannot account for the disappearance of their son, Louis, the Dauphin, from his prison but agrees that he, too, escaped the guillotine.

King Louis XVI, himself, was not aware of the threat of events hurdling down on him and he desperately tried to avert the avalanche of hatred crushing on his regency by agreeing to some of the early demands of the Estates General.

Although the revolution was constantly being fed by the blood of the innocent the drunken frenzy of the Parisian mob demanded evermore of it.

The rural people of France were slow to realize what was happening to them. Only when tragedy struck their own province did they understand and respond. It was usually too little and too late.

There were heroes who arose to fight these revolutionaries and were the greater for their efforts.

For many of the French people a resolve to restore and start a new life elsewhere took hold in their hearts. This is the story of one such hero, Jean Paul DeBrosse.

❧

WILD IS THE WIND - RICHARD LOUIS FEDERER

Wild is the Wind

Oh, wild is the wind
Of a following sea
That beckons me search
For my lost love, Marie

From halyards to mizzenmast
I've oft heard her sigh
Bemoaning her sorrow
To a star studded sky

O, she'll scream in a gale
And loose every shroud
I once heard her weeping
But never out loud

From taffrail to bowsprit
From foremast to main
She'll never stop singing
Her plain song refrain

O, come home me darlin'
O, come home to me
Abandon your love
For the following sea

-By Richard Louis Federer

Midway down the west coast of France,
near where the Loire River runs into the Bay of Biscay,
is an area called the hedge country, or "the Bocage."

CHAPTER 1

From the town of Melun to the city of Paris is a distance of 28 miles. In the summer of 1793 it was a hot, dusty, suffocating trip by highway coach down the Seine river road, or a cooler, slower and more expensive trip by river coach down the Seine itself. The fastest way was by horseback though it was a sweaty ride often choking with dust.

To seventeen year old Jean Paul DeBrosse it was a trip without options. He had to sell his family's horse in La Rochelle when a gang of 'citizen' ruffians had belabored him with words and then clubs and rocks for his black sheep-skinned saddle, a distinctive mark of the French Bocage farmers since the days of Charles Martel, grandfather of Charlemagne who in 732 stopped the Muslim hordes from conquering all of France at the Battle of Tours, a city ten leagues distance from Jean Paul's home.

The loss of his horse occurred on the road to Nantes. Jean Paul had ridden through a makeshift barricade when out from the brush near the road six revolutionaries grabbed his reins and pulled him to the ground. They wanted his horse, especially his black sheep skin saddle, to show to the commander of the revolutionary guard in the city of Nantes. Jean Paul agreed to part with the horse but demanded payment for the saddle.

One gang member tossed him a five livre note for the saddle knowing that the troop commander in Nantes would send soldiers later to capture the lad. Once the commander saw the saddle, the livre note would soon be back in the ruffian's pocket, or so they thought. They did not appreciate Jean Paul's skill in hiding in the Bocage once the troops were after him.

Located fifty miles south of Nantes, the Bocage country, as the peasants called it, was impenetrable to pass because each field and pasture was bound on four sides by thick hedgerows of trees, brush and earthworks at least four feet high. Once, when Jean Paul was young, he lost his way in the pasture and spent a desperate day and a half trying to find his way back home.

"Always travel north by west," his older brother Henri cautioned, "that way you'll eventually find a road." Jean Paul sobbed his assent in his mother's breast and vowed never to get lost again.

Strangers to the country seldom ventured into the Bocage. The French government referred to the area as the Vendee and paid little attention to it, a decision they would come to rue.

But Jean Paul loved the countryside, hopelessly rural as it was. If he were poor, he didn't know it. All of the Vendeans were poor. If he were uneducated he didn't care.

The works of Rousseau and Voltaire never reached south of the Loire river and certainly not into the Bocage.

Each little estate had its own church where on Sundays the local Cure' brought the news of Christ and the news of the surrounding countryside to the Vendeans.

Besides, the Christian Brothers had founded a school for teenage boys in his hometown of Saint Florient-le-Vieil, as they did all over France. Unlike the Jesuits, a more intellectual order, the Christian Brothers, none of whom were priests, taught no Latin or Greek, little history or government, but instead taught draftsmanship, mathematics, navigation, simple accounting and a deep love for their religion and language. The courses were designed to teach thousands of French peasants the skills necessary to carry on the businesses of their fathers and to serve the upper class.

It was too bad that the Revolutionaries had not been educated by the Christian Brothers. Perhaps then they would not have made two severe blunders in the handling of the Vendee crisis.

The two blunders of the French Revolutionary Convention were the immediate causes of the Vendee uprising. The first blunder was the declaration of war against all of the European powers; Prussia, Austria, Belgium, England, and Spain. That burst of revolutionary fervor exported their radical ideas to the whole known western world. One of their ideas, the killing of one's king, was supposed to be a great leap towards liberty, but the monarchies of Europe were not so inclined to accept this view. In fact, they readily accepted war with France in large measure to defend their own heads and crowns.

At all events, France needed 300,000 men to flesh out their army to fight the wars they started. Conscription of the non-revolutionaries seemed to be the quickest way to achieve this.

The Vendeans had refused to be drafted to fight a war for a group of radicals who had murdered their king, Louis XVI, and had exiled their priests.

It was more than they could stomach.

Secondly, this same radical group that had exiled all their priests and closed their churches tried to make the peasants swear an oath abjuring their pope and their religion. And so on March 12, 1793 on the town square of Saint Florient-le-Vieil, two thousand Bocage farmers suddenly appeared to challenge the Revolutionary National Guard with their rakes, clubs, shotguns and scythes. Two weeks before this fatal day in March, rumors spread from man to man that a delegation from Paris was approaching Saint Florient-le-Vieil to draft and impress young Frenchmen into the Revolutionary Army. Word was passed to meet at the Vendean churches for instructions on how to fight and what weapons to use.

Jean Paul was designated communications soldier, responsible for relaying the message from church to church. He could travel light and knew the Bocage well. He would be in charge of rousing the northern part of the Vendee.

By March 12, 1793, the reception for the Paris radicals was complete. Silently for an hour the peasants gathered in Saint Florient's Square. At the appointed hour, the square became full. Jean Paul was there in the front row brandishing his reaping scythe and crying out "Vive le Roi" and "Vive le bonnes pères" with the crowd.

Suddenly, a shot rang out from someone in the square. It was aimed at the Parisian officials and the members of the Revolutionary Guard. One guard fell clutching his belly.

At that, the soldiers leveled their muskets on the crowd and fired. Immediately, four Vendeans fell dead, one at the feet of Jean Paul, a bullet through his forehead. Forty more peasants fell wounded. At that, a general mêlée began as the peasants rushed the platform *enmasse*. It took a full minute for the guards to reload their muskets, much too long to stop the peasant's headlong rush toward the platform. Seeing this rush of humanity, the Revolutionaries broke formation and ran. Some dropped their muskets, which were immediately picked up by the peasants. This scavenging for the weapons, allowed the soldiers more time to escape to a small island in the Loire River. The bloody uprising of the Vendee had begun.

What began as a small uprising grew into the most horrible purge of the French Revolution. The purge became known as "The Terror", the bloodiest year of the entire French Revolution, culminating in the deaths of forty thousand Parisians and Frenchmen by club, sword, pike, and guillotine. To this day the "Age of Terror" is irrevocably linked to the people of Paris and the French Revolution.

Celebration soon broke out as the Vendeans, stunned by their sudden victory, congratulated themselves with copious draughts of wine. The commander of the motley army was shocked by the quick success of his efforts. At the Inn on the far side of the square Jean Paul was toasted as a hero.

A man from the Royal Catholic Army of Vendee approached Jean Paul and offered him a commission on the spot.

Jean Paul declined the offer but took the man's name anyway.

When Jean Paul heard the other uprisings had occurred spontaneously in other Bocage towns on the same day, he decided to uproot his life and find a cavalry outfit he could join. He did not have to travel far, for fifteen miles south an uprising led by a 33-year old baker named Jacques Castelineau had gathered a thousand Bocage men riding horses saddled in black sheep-skins. They captured two cannons and four towns.

Jean Paul eagerly joined the group. Commander and trooper were made for each other.

His first mission for Castelineau was to ride to all the generals, now four, in the Vendee and tell them to press on to more towns, capture them and stockpile the captured weapons. This the generals did with great dispatch. The armies moved against the Revolutionary Guard with such fervor that they captured most of the Vendee within two weeks. Paris was aghast with this success. Even Robespierre, one of the main leaders of the French Revolution, was haunted by the prospect of this uprising spoiling or perhaps destroying his revolution.

General Castelineau desperately needed to know of the counterattack plans that this lightning, *coup de foudre*, had attracted in Paris. Young Jean Paul could certainly find out especially through his contacts with the Christian Brothers at the Motherhouse in Melun.

Within a week, Jean Paul kissed his ma mère goodbye and headed north on the King's highway. He could not have known that his mother's kiss would be the last act of love she would ever give him.

Twice Jean Paul had spied his mother digging at the stonemasonry wall with a kitchen knife. She was attempting to cut away the bousilage that covered the stone walls in the small cabin.

The French were known to hide their valuables in the risers of a staircase or in the plaster chinks in their cabin walls.

Jean Paul knew she wanted to give him the few coins she had saved for his trip to Paris.

"No, Mother, no," Jean Paul admonished, "I can make it without your money, but may I borrow the horse? I'll be back within a month." He pecked a kiss on her tear-stained cheek

Jean Paul kissed his ma mère goodbye,
not knowing that he would never see her again.

and was gone.

As *courier du bois*, a traveler of the woods for Castelineau, young Jean Paul pondered on these things as he struggled with his pack. He was still five miles from Melun and the welcoming arms of his teacher and mentor, Brother Aloysius Benoit, a Belgian Christian Brother. Brother Benoit loved his students and Jean Paul, in particular, or so Jean Paul thought. For several years prior to the outbreak of war in the Vendee, it was customary for the Brothers to return each summer to their Motherhouse at Melun for rest and updates on the French hotbed of revolution in Paris.

Now that he was closing in on Melun, Jean Paul knew that Paris was not far away and he must be especially careful of spies and the Convention Committee members of the Revolution who were looking for any deviation from the approved code of conduct for members of the Revolutionary Society.

He had replaced his head cap, a nondescript woolen affair, with a red cap and adorned it with a tricolor cockade instead of the white cockade of the king of France; he slashed his pants off at the knees so that his dress was 'sans culottes' and not breeches of the gentry; he doctored his speech by addressing everyone as 'citizen' not Monsieur, Madam or Mademoiselle, as his mother had taught him and he averted his eyes so that no one could see the sorrow and shock he felt when passing churches and cathedrals whose statues had been broken or ripped from their doorway niches.

The closer he drew toward Melun and the outskirts of Paris, the more he felt the hatred of the people toward all manifestations of religious belief. He knew he was entering the realm of the ungodly.

Determined not to tell anyone of his true mission to
Paris, Jean Paul informed his friends and allies that he was on a
mission for General Castelineau, for that indeed, was his current
mission in the Royal Catholic Army of the Vendee. As courier
du bois, he carried messages to and from the Generals of the
Vendee army. He had been selected, he recalled, because of
his youth, his riding ability, and his knowledge of the Bocage.
Though he was large and well-formed for a boy of seventeen,
one would not think that a lad his age would be entrusted with
such an important duty.

Jean Paul was quick and clever and his piercing black
eyes noticed and recorded everything. General Castelineau
knew that if the uprising in the Vendee lasted two or more
years, Jean Paul's frame would support a very muscular man
possibly reaching six feet tall. This was beneficial to the war
effort because Jean Paul could pass as either a peasant or a
Parisian. Frenchmen born in the north of France had plenty of
height, almost Prussian, whereas those born in southern France,
although strong as an oak tree, were prone to be short and
stocky. Castelineau knew he had chosen well.

When the General sent Jean Paul to Paris, he did not
know of the secret mission that Jean Paul had chosen for himself.

He was under the impression that the boy would discover
the counterattack plans to Castelineau's uprising. Jean Paul had
other ideas as well and he would perfect his plans in Melun
under the guise of visiting his old friend, Brother Benoit.

But for now, Jean Paul was only thinking of Charlotte
Corday and her bold strike against Marat, one of the
Revolutionary architects.

No man in France possessed the raw courage of Charlotte
Corday, a tall, slender, highly intelligent French woman who

held John Paul Marat personally responsible for all of France's evil days. She resolved to remove him with one stroke of a blade to the heart. What she did not realize was the French Revolution was like a seven-headed Hydra of ancient Greek legend; cut off one head and six remain to attack you. Marat was just one head and a minor one at that.

With a single-minded purpose she calmly bought a kitchen knife in the market place, walked to Marat's house, gained an audience with him, still soaking in his daily bath, by informing his manservant that she had the names of anti-Revolutionaries on her person. When the servant left the room she presented the list to Marat and while he perused it, she coldly stabbed him in the heart. She, of course, was caught and within a few days was beheaded. Such courage inflamed French hearts, none more so than Jean Paul DeBrosse.

Jean Paul had barely finished this reverie of Charlotte Corday, when his eyes caught a glimpse of Melun, which turned his attention back to the task at hand.

As he drew closer to the town, the Motherhouse of the Christian Brothers of France lay squarely in the middle of an island, surrounded by the Seine River. Planted solidly on the outskirts of Melun, the Motherhouse proudly stood three stories tall. Formerly a convent for the Ursuline nuns it seemed to soar above all the houses in the town like a queen surrounded by her court. Her slate roof was firmly anchored by a fretwork of cast iron snow guards that ran the length the roof. The wrought iron gates protected the well dressed garden beyond. Jean Paul gazed in amazement. He felt the strength of the structure that seemed to announce,

"Here I am and here I stand."

He could hardly wait to run to Brother Benoit's approving

embrace and steal the wooden canes from his cincture, those old, sawed off, wooden walking sticks that had been a source of discipline during his formative years. Brother Benoit would walk the aisles of his classroom and crack any student caught nodding off to sleep. Jean Paul's classmates fondly named them Split and Splat.

Jean Paul could hardly wait to see the stables of the Christian Brothers' motherhouse where he had been told, Jeanne d'Arc herself had entrusted her own horse before entering the Melun Cathedral on her triumphant journey to Paris. Oh, it would be a grand reunion.

His mind was still lost in his childhood memories as he clanged the porter's bell three times before a lone black cassocked figure approached the gate. It then became ominously quiet.

Looking nervously from side to side the small man made his way to the front gate. "You from Paris?" he questioned as his fingers nervously fumbled with the keys.

"No, no" replied Jean Paul, "I'm from the Bocage, here to see Brother Benoit, my teacher."

"Oh, oh, alright," the short man replied beckoning him forward,

"Hurry, it is not safe to be seen outside the house. Follow me quickly."

The old brother turned away suddenly, forgetting to lock the front gate. Jean Paul pointed to the lock. "Oh yes, yes, I must lock it."

No other sound passed between them till they had entered the refectory.

Once inside the dining room the small Brother ventured, "By the way, I am Brother Marcuse."

Cathedral in Melun, France

"And I am Jean Paul DeBrosse," added Jean Paul completing the introduction.

"Would you care for a cup of water, a glass of wine?" rejoined Brother Marcuse. "We have a little Bordeaux left."

Safe inside the cool, cavernous dining room, Jean Paul allowed himself a respite from the tension of his pilgrimage and began to relax.

"Whatever is coolest to drink," he responded unloading his sack on a chair.

"Let's make it Bordeaux, then." Brother Marcuse responded with authority and reached for a decanter placed on the credenza conveniently behind him.

While the good brother was filling the plain crystal glasses, Jean Paul surveyed the room. Though most of the furniture had been removed it was easy to imagine a hundred or so brothers gathering quietly for an evening repast within its spacious dimensions. The walls were smooth, white plaster, and ten feet high. Except for the occasional black horsehair that bound the white plaster together they were unrelieved by any pictures, statues or crosses of any kind.

Looking carefully at the wall above the massive stone fireplace, Jean Paul could detect the faint outline of a great crucifix whose sooty shadow had not been sufficiently scrubbed off.

Noticing Jean Paul's gaze toward the fireplace Brother Marcuse remarked somberly, "Oh, that…that. We tried our best, but the Committee invaded the house so fast we barely had time to remove the crucifix before they were on us. They smashed all of the other pictures and statues and were preparing to leave when one of them spotted the outline on the wall where the crucifix once hung. The brutes ransacked the chapel until they uncovered the crucifix in the sanctuary. We understand it was taken to Paris as evidence against us."

"So Brother Benoit is not here?" questioned the lad.

Brother Marcuse responded, "No, he rushed to Paris. Brother Simoneau was arrested...I don't know what for...we heard he is imprisoned at Saint-Sulpice. Brother Benoit, left shortly after the break-in, disguised as an itinerant tradesman, in the hopes of retrieving him."

Shocked by the news, Jean Paul responded, "I thought only priests and nuns were being arrested. Everyone knows the Brothers are not priests. They only teach the poor of France."

"That was true last week," replied Brother Marcuse, "They started taking members of the royalty and killing them. Next, it was the rich and the bourgeoisie middle class who lost their heads. Finally, it was anyone who espoused the Christian faith. Now, the Committee of Public Safety does not even require an arrest warrant, just the word from any Revolutionary is enough to lose your head.

No indictment, no proof, no evidence and when they ask whether you abjure the faith, if you answer, 'no', your fate is sealed."

After a brief moment, Brother Marcuse continued, "I heard last week, of two women, who though unrelated, bore the same last name. Rather than finding out who was the indicted one, the Revolutionaries cut off the heads of both of them."

"Is this the work of Robespierre?" questioned Jean Paul, "Should not someone kill that monster?" Jean Paul fell silent and flashed a searching look at the window.

"Two thousand heads a month are cut off at the Place de la Revolution," muttered the brother sadly, "I fear for both

Rioting mobs in France ransacked churches.

of their lives."

Without a moment's hesitation, Jean Paul declared, "Then I must go at once!"

"You are just a lad, my son," returned Brother Marcuse, "you know nothing of this satanic evil."

"Oh, I have seen blood, Brother," remarked Jean Paul rising from the chair to his full height, "I was an aide to Castelineau when he set the Vendee free from Robespierre's grip. I was sent here to find out when the Revolutionaries will counterattack." With a blank stare fixed firmly on Brother Marcuse he continued, "I am not afraid of death, Brother."

I am sure you are not," replied the elderly Brother Marcuse quietly. He was proud to see courage in one so young, "but tyrannicide demands more than courage, my son."

"Like what?" questioned Jean Paul sharply.

"Well, for one thing, Mother Church insists that the leader of the nation one wishes to kill be a monster who rules by cruelty, death and unrelenting terror unrelieved by any chance of change by law or civil means. If his death would bring an end to this conduct and return peace and sanity to the government then perhaps we are allowed to abrogate Jesus' statement, 'Vengeance is mine, saith the Lord'."

Brother Marcuse stopped for a long breath, looking deeply into Jean Paul's confused face, "But Brother Benoit is the authority on tyrannicide. I am not."

"Perhaps I should talk to Brother Benoit," said Jean Paul.

"Perhaps," added Brother Marcuse as he turned to pour more wine, "but in any event Louie, King of France is already dead."

"But the monster is not!" added Jean Paul.

Brother Marcuse turned back on Jean Paul. He did not understand. "Oh, if only they had not exiled all our brothers and priests," mused Brother Marcuse, "they could explain this problem to you more fully."

"But you have, Brother, you have," returned Jean Paul, enthusiastically. "I must go now," Jean Paul concluded rising from his chair.

"Wait," interrupted Brother Marcuse, "I am on friendly terms with one of the river coachmen. I can get you transportation as far as Corbeil, at least. Rest awhile and I will make the necessary arrangements."

Jean Paul wanted to continue the conversation. He especially wanted to probe the good Brother's memory to find the whereabouts of Robespierre's residence and the Rue d' Abattoir. These were critical to his plans.

"By the way Brother, do you know where Robespierre lives?"

It was too late Brother Marcuse had already left the room.

≪

Boat on the Seine River, which flows through Paris.

CHAPTER 2

Though Jean Paul had never been to sea he had spent much time on the Loire River. He knew enough about boats from keel to cordelle mast to enjoy himself when on his favorite perch, the taffrail behind the helmsman. At that spot, he had the best view of the boat and the entire country ahead.

He enjoyed it all especially talking to the helmsman whose squinty left eye told him he had spent much time at sea, traveling into the western sunset; it had surely blinded him. The bandana over the right eye was the classic mark of a seasoned helmsman, and was meant to preserve whatever vision was left.

"I'm called Georges," announced the scruffy dressed helmsman nodding towards Jean Paul.

"I'm Jean Paul," responded the lad, "from the Vendee."

"Oh," drawled Georges knowingly.

"It wasn't just the western course that made my eye blind," continued the old seaman, "Oh, everyone wants to know how I lost it…To find your latitude you poked your eye through this peephole lined with bits of black glass and stare at the sun above the horizon to find the amount of degrees it lies above the ocean. You give the degrees to your navigator and he calculates your position on the earth. The peephole is called a Back Staff and you can go blind using it. Then, you're finished with the sea."

Sextant used by sailors to find their latitude at sea.

Jean Paul nodded knowingly, but he could not completely know.

Today they were traveling mostly north on the Seine River, so the helmsman had time to talk even though the snaky Seine would "box the compass" on its way to Paris.

The sun was setting when the *Blade-de-Roi* left Melun heading towards Paris. The rivercoach was not much more than a glorified barge but it served its purpose. The boat consisted of three dismounted carriages firmly affixed to a wooden grain barge, mounting a single mast on the top of which was fastened an iron ring through which a pulling rope was passed.

The ungainly looking rivercoach used neither sail nor oar to make its way upriver.

Sunset on the Seine River.

The whole assembly was called a cordelle. When the boat was going against the river's current, men would walk along the river on a foot path hauling the cordelle rope over their shoulders. It was slow, tedious work but it did move the vessel upriver. But now they were going downstream and the cordelle crew was not needed.

Jean Paul felt the cool evening breeze against his face and it gave his mind a chance to plan the future.

The rivercoach had barely left the Melun dock when from the opposite shore came shouts of "Service….Service, citizen."

The helmsman pulled the steering oar hard to port, letting the Seine current slowly push the boat to a nose-in landing on the shore. Three rough looking men wearing tricolor cockades forcefully herded a finely dressed gentleman in silk breeches, his elegantly dressed wife, and their two young daughters on board the boat.

They were rushed, half stumbling into the first carriage

where the blinds were quickly drawn. Two citizen guards stood outside the door.

As the family was climbing into the carriage, the youngest daughter, perhaps fourteen years of age, spied Jean Paul. Their eyes met for the briefest of moments, and Jean Paul stunned by her beauty, froze in place. A man's voice broke the spell, "Angelique Marie!" It was a moment that Jean Paul would never forget.

"I'll bet they're captured émigrés trying to escape the death machine in Paris," whispered Georges in a low voice, "Those rough looking citizens are bounty hunters and from the looks of their prisoners those émigrés could be royalty, at least till their heads come off."

He grinned a toothless grin.

"Even the children?" questioned Jean Paul.

"Oh yes," Georges replied, "They be first....early in the morning, the Committee doesn't want any *enfants* to remember the work of the blade and the blood. If you admire any such children...better look fast for they'll be beheaded in a day or two."

Jean Paul fell silent. His mind was numbed by the prospect of never again seeing the coquettish twinkle in the eyes of the younger girl, or the softer, deeper eyes of her older sister.

Jean Paul drew his hands into his pockets, feeling the coins he had been paid for selling his family's horse and shrugged his shoulders. After a long while he spoke, "If we could save them, could you smuggle them back to Brother Marcuse at the motherhouse in Melun?"

"All of them?" inquired Georges nervously.

"I could pay you," returned Jean Paul.

Then noticing Georges' concerned look, continued, "Well, the young ones, at least."

"You'll come with me, then?" pushed Georges.

"I have a rendezvous in Paris. I must be there," confided Jean Paul.

"Let me see your money then," demanded Georges squinting his weathered eye.

Jean Paul felt the coins in his pocket and carefully withdrew some sous and livres, holding back enough money to purchase a knife, preferably a dirk, and perhaps enough livres to buy passage down the Seine from Paris to Honfleur and the sea. He carefully counted out the coins into Georges' hand.

"C'est bon," Georges nodded, "Now, at dinner tonight you'll bring some porridge and wine to the fine gentleman's carriage, extra wine for the guards, of course, and while serving the family you'll explain the plan to them."

The scruffy old helmsman continued, "I'll fill two sea bags with junk, like wood and scraps and weighty stuff to throw overboard. At two bells tonight, arouse the girls and have them make plenty of noise.

Instruct them to run back to me and I'll slip them into the boat locker and close the lock. Then we will throw the sea bags overboard as if the girls are jumping into the Seine.

Then, on my return trip, I will let them out of the lockers and deliver them to the monastery."

"What about the parents?" questioned Jean Paul.

"Ha! How about the whole city of Paris?" joked Georges.

Jean Paul pressed, "If I can get their parents free from the prison of Saint Sulpice can you smuggle them back to the Motherhouse at Melun? I will pay you for it."

"Look, I turn around at Versailles. That will give you three days to have them at the city dock for a return trip. If they are there in the morning of the third day, I will take them. If not, they walk!" stated Georges.

"Good," returned Jean Paul, "Tell Brother Marcuse to pay you what you require. He knows me well and knows that I will pay him back when I return to Melun."

At six o'clock, Jean Paul heated the canister of porridge and scooped four bowls of it into some soupcons, and carried them precariously toward Coach Number One. He did not know if his nervousness was the result of his fright of the impending adventure or the realization that he would soon meet the two beauties his dark eyes remembered. Either way he was thrilled by the excitement.

When he arrived at Coach Number One, he first tendered three bottles of wine to the thirsty guards who were immediately distracted from the game afoot. He took a deep breath and opened the coach door. A waiter, Jean Paul was not, but he managed to serve the porridge and a bottle of wine to his patrons without spilling a drop.

He did all of this while his gaze was riveted on the two girls; each different in their own way but equally charming.

The older girl appeared to be made of delicate Dresden china. She looked as regal and delicate as the powder puff statue on his mother's dresser with long slender fingers, soft brown eyes, perfectly coiffed hair and carefully lined lips. Her name was Clare Louise.

Her younger sister was Angelique Marie, the blonde, vivacious, athletic charmer, who caught his attention when they first boarded. As Jean Paul served the soup to Angelique Marie, he notice her hands. They had known the reins of a horse and Jean Paul sensed that it would be difficult to keep up with her.

The older sister, Clare Louise, and younger sister, Angelique Marie, quickly boarded the boat headed toward Paris.

She spoke quickly and flashed her light blue eyes searching for agreement, "Will you help us? Will you save us from these monsters?"

Within seconds, Jean Paul delivered the escape plan to their parents. He apologized that he could only save the girls at this time, but their parents were grateful for his help anyway. They assured their daughters that they, too, would find a way to escape, somehow.

As he finished his instructions, Jean Paul he looked each girl in the eyes and instinctively knew he would marry one of them, but he knew not which one. No sooner had he finished, then the guards pulled him out of the coach.

At 2:00 a.m., with the drunken guards fast asleep, Jean Paul and Georges put their plan to work. It all went spectacularly, except that in the excitement Jean Paul thought that the sea bags did not make enough noise. He could hear only one bag hit the water so without thinking he jumped overboard causing a horrendous splash screaming, "Angelique Marie!"

The drowsy guards believed that all three had jumped off the boat, Angelique Marie, Clare Louise, and Jean Paul.

They assumed that all three would drown in the dark, frigid waters. Those stupid children will die within minutes. They would have less to worry about.

Jean Paul hit the cold river water, and began frantically swimming, looking for the shoreline. He did not think before he acted, and now he realized that he may never see them again.

"What am I doing? The girls are still onboard!"

The *Blade-de-Roi* was now a quarter mile downstream from Jean Paul, and a few nautical miles from the outskirts of Paris. As the cold water took hold of his limbs, he slowly swam toward the shore, hoping for warmth and better luck.

On board, safely in a cramped boat locker, the girls could hear Georges explaining to the guards that he could not put about and go upstream for he had no cordelle footmen to pull the boat against the current unless, of course, the guards were willing to do so. They were not.

When the river coach arrived at the water dock in Paris, Monsieur and Madame DuPrey were quickly hustled ashore and marched over the rough cobblestones to Saint Sulpice, the church turned prison, where they were duly enrolled as the latest prisoners to enter the jail. They were entered in the book as *riche bourgeoisie*.

Monsieur DuPrey was delighted to note that the clerk in charge had to turn almost a dozen pages of his prison register before he found a clean page on which to make his newest entry. This meant, that the they had at least one-half week of victims names ahead of the DuPreys before the court docket reached their names.

Monsieur DuPrey took his wife's hand and led her to a corner bench in the front of the church where they could find some privacy. There he explained their good fortune and began to outline a plan of escape.

First, they must disabuse their finery by ripping their clothes and stockings and removing their wigs and other adornments so that that they blended in more with the Parisian population. The gold coins which Madame Duprey had sewn into the hem of her skirt were cut out and placed in her shoes.

Monsieur DuPrey noticed that a guard near the prison door was counting what appeared to be coins. He would test the guard by offering a few coins for bread and wine. If this worked he would, at a later date, try to bribe an escape with this man. It did not matter if he was found out. No one left Saint Sulpice with his head intact anyway.

"Monsieur," he began when the moment was ripe, "a bottle of wine and some bread?"

He held out his hand offering two gold pieces.

❧

CHAPTER 3

Paris was beautiful this time of year, Jean Paul thought to himself as he strode down the nearly deserted Champs Elysee. His clothes were still damp from his unfortunate early morning swim in the Seine River, but as the sun slowly warmed, the wetness began to dry off. The three hundred foot wide boulevard was as yet unpaved in 1793 but it was flanked on both sides by six rows of oak trees now turning gold in the sun.

Jean Paul had been walking toward Paris in his wet clothes since dawn making only one detour on the outskirts of the city; the Rue d' Abattoir. This was the street that led to the slaughterhouse where the animals were butchered in the city.

The bleating of the sheep and the bellowing of the cattle led him through narrow, winding, medieval streets to a series of open pens where the doomed were taken before slaughter. Were the doomed of the revolution so carefully watched and groomed before their death?

As Jean Paul mulled over the events of the past hours, he walked carelessly into one of the back streets of the Rue d' Abattoir, running into a butcher near the meat market.

"Hey, citizen, what can I do for you?" questioned the

Bridge crossimg the Seine River in Paris.

grisly, blood- spackled man.

"I be lookin' fur a butcher knife…a dirk, maybe," answered Jean Paul faking a naval swagger.

"That far too much blade for butcherin', but you might try the knife shack across the alley," he suggested.

"Merci," responded Jean Paul and he nonchalantly ambled down the alley. As he turned the corner the shine of a polished blade caught his eye. That was his blade!

"You after vengeance?" chuckled the old woman shopkeeper as she handed the dirk over to Jean Paul. He grinned in tacit agreement at the old snaggletooth hag.

"Got to defend yourself these days," answered Jean Paul slapping the livres she wanted on the wooden counter and sauntered off.

"Do you want a scabbard?" shouted the old woman.

Without turning around Jean Paul shook his head no and pointed to the sash around his waist.

At last, he thought, he was on the great road to his destiny.

Although Jean Paul was more than a mile and a half away he could clearly see the gathering crowd scurrying into the *Place de la Revolution*. It was here that the death machine, the guillotine, held court.

How could people who live in such a beautiful country, he wondered, who admired grace and beauty, trade all this for the blood of its citizens? It was a phenomenon he could not accept. Nevertheless, his feet plodded forward to the Revolutionary Square.

He had to see for himself the great horror that was demanding his soul to kill the perpetrator of this evil.

Unlike Rome, Paris was not noted for its public squares, at least not prior to the sixteenth century.

Its streets were narrow, winding and cluttered with people, dogs, carts, sedan chairs, men on horseback, priests, and peddlers of all kinds. The clutter of people and trash was so bad that Louis XIV, commonly referred to as Louis Quatorze, refused to live in Paris and moved his court to Versailles.

At that time, he also began the construction of the famous squares in Paris. There were five of them: *Place Dauphin*, *Place Royale*, now called *Vosges*, *Place de Vendome*, *Place de la Victories* and *Place de Louis XV*, renamed *Place de la Revolution* in 1789, eventually settling with the name *Place de la Concorde.*

The squares were created to showcase the statues of royalty, past and present, as well as provide a place for the populace to visit and hold concourse with their neighbors. In 1789, after the fall of the Bastille, the ancient prison of Paris, the people of Paris marched to Versailles and placed the king and queen under arrest. Taking them back to Paris, the noble prisoners were lodged in a building called the Tuileries where they stayed until their beheading in the *Place de la Revolution.*

It was here on January 21, 1793, before 20,000 armed guards and 100,000 people of Paris who crammed the streets and flooded the public square that Louis XVI was publicly beheaded by the guillotine. The beginning of this blood letting did not end until more than a decade later.

Jean Paul entered the square and was immediately met by an overwhelming stench; a combination of besotted drunkards, fresh and dried blood, and horse manure.

It was not yet noon but the crowd was noticeably drunk. No one seemed to care.

"You should have been here yesterday…now that was a real drinking group," offered a fortyish year old man steadying himself on Jean Paul's shoulder.

"They only got fifty-seven of 'em today and they are all Christians, and to think that today used to be a Sunday," he muttered smugly.

The old man was referring to the fact that the Revolutionary Convention had changed the seven-day week to a ten-day week displacing Sunday to Wednesday. The months were renamed also.

Jean Paul nodded silently and began pushing himself deeper into the crowd, nearly to the front. He could now get a sense of the scale of the death machine. It rested on a platform six feet high and from there it rose twelve feet more.

Its two inch thick blade was pierced by a hole at the back of the blade through which a rope was carefully knotted. When hauled up to its full height the rope would fall over the top of the machine and down its side where it was secured to a wooden cleat.

The guillotine was manned by four men, one who assisted the victim up the twelve steps to the platform. Often those steps were slippery with blood. Once on the platform the headsman would bind the victim's hands behind their backs.

After the execution he would retrieve the severed head from the catching basket and hold it up for the cheering crowd to see.

Because the heart of the victim would continue pumping, blood would splatter the headsman, the platform, staircase and any citizen who ventured too close to the blade.

The sight of the blood smeared hands, face, and wildly unkempt beard of the horrible headsman burned itself into the memory of Jean Paul so deeply that he would never, ever forget him.

The two laconic sliders would take the unsuspecting victim from the headsman and turn him toward the front of the machine, flipping him on the sliding board facedown and pushing his head through the 'widow's hole'.

The sliders worked efficiently and quietly, never looking at their victim's face or the crowd.

The executioner would unwind the rope from around the restraining cleat and let the rope fly loose. In less than four seconds the blade did its gruesome work.

Everyone knew the workings of the machine and so they turned their attention to the victim and the "devil dance of death" that was performed. After showing the head to the crowd, it would be picked up and placed on a pike held by one of the ruffians who stood near the steps. He would then run through the jeering crowd as the macabre dance wound its way through the streets of Paris where the gruesome trophy was placed on a post or fence for all to behold.

Suddenly, there was a commotion at the west gate of the square. It seemed that the horses pulling a tumbrel full of doomed citizens refused to enter the square.

"They smell the stale blood from yesterday or maybe this morning," suggested a mustached old man. "I saw this once on a bloodied battlefield...Horses are smart. They know death when they smell it."

Others nodded in agreement. The pavement, mostly wooden blocks, had been soaked with blood for weeks.

Even the dogs that lapped the blood every night had their fill of the orgy.

Finally, the horses had enough of the whiplashing and the cart came into view. At first, Jean Paul could only make out what appeared to be several large white birds bobbing their heads on the top rail of the cart. He looked around questioningly. He did not have to wait long for an answer.

"Why they're God's Geese, the Daughters of Charity. They run the hospital. I'd know their headpieces anywhere!" exclaimed a heavyset woman pressing her folded hands to her pursed lips, "What will we do without them?"

As each nun hopped down from the cart, the eldest one, presumably the Mother Superior removed the nun's white

Beheading in Paris.

coronettes from their heads with these words, "By God's grace you were given these wings, and to God's grace you must now fly."

She quickly kissed their cheeks and just as quickly they each climbed, in turn, up the twelve steps to the platform looking neither to the right or left and obediently presented their hands to be bound by the headsman.

In fifteen minutes the entire gaggle of God's Geese had flown to heaven. Jean Paul was stunned. He was in shock. After the first execution, he had placed his hand over his left eye so that the full horror of the scene would be partially blocked from his mind's eye.

His right eye was now wet with either tears or blood. He knew not which, but reached into his pocket for a handkerchief to wipe the wet from his face.

The cheer, "Vive la Republique, Vive la Nation" was still ringing in his ears when Jean Paul decided he had seen enough and turned to leave when a second tumbril creaked into view. It was full of men this time, clinging to the top rail of the cart in desperation, all except one dressed in a black cassock standing straight and erect at the tail of the wagon.

Jean Paul had seen that face, admired that face and loved that face for years. It was Brother Aloysius Benoit.

A torrent of questions battered his brain: how, who, why, all competed for answers. Robespierre would have to wait, he thought, he must witness this drama.

Jean Paul knew the satanic ritual by now. Only this time he would watch with both eyes open, recording every second.

At the end of it he considered charging the machine with his dirk to slay, at least, the grimacing headsman who had noticed him from the previous executions.

Cart carrying victims off to be beheaded by the guillotine.

The dignity and reserve of Brother Benoit was a joy to behold, Jean Paul thought. He was magnificent in death.

Without thinking, Jean Paul slowly traced the sign of the cross over his face and shoulders, something his mother taught him to do, whenever witnessing a holy act of God. He knew immediately that he had been observed.

In fact, the headsman eyes had locked on him from the start of Brother Benoit's execution.

"Seize him!" cried the headsman, "Grab the boy, he's a Christian! Seize him!"

A cannon blast could not have exploded louder in Jean Paul's ears. He knew the shouting was leveled at him. Without a moment's hesitation, he bolted through the crowd.

The screams of, "Catch him! Seize him! Hold him! Don't let him escape!" echoed through the square.

Jean Paul's speed was too much for the drunken crowd. He wiggled, twisted, and slithered his way past the grabbing hands until he found the gate where his young legs could prove his youth. He was free; nothing in the world could catch him now.

Jean Paul was at least a hundred yards ahead of the following crowd when he spotted a fish cart parked alongside the boulevard. These carts were used to transport the fresh catch from the fishing boats berthed at the town of Honfleur to the royal Tuileries Palace. The cart horses were the fastest in the country for they had to carry the local catch 100 miles from the sea to banquet halls before the fish spoiled.

The horses were unhitched now, but the cart still contained a huge barrel tied to one corner of the wagon.

It was big enough to hide him. He climbed aboard the open bed of the cart and scrambled into the barrel. The empty

"Seize him!" cried the headsman, "Grab the boy,
he's a Christian! Seize him!"

barrel smelled of salt water and fish, but with his life at stake, he
could stand the sickening stench for awhile. After a few minutes
the crowd of young boys and men passed him by flinging
curses and profanities after their lost quarry.

Contemplating life in a fish barrel was not what Jean
Paul had in mind, but the pressure of his present circumstance
left him no alternative.

Fingering his dirk, he knew that as a wanted man, killing
Robespierre was quite impossible.

It was silly of him to think that he could, by himself,
ever do such a thing. He would never be so foolish again.

Well, at least, he thought, he saved the lives of two

girls. A tear broke from his eyes when he remembered his failure to save Brother Benoit.

As the day wore on, Jean Paul's mind could not help but review the day's horror; the slaughter of God's Geese, the courage of Brother Benoit, and the description of the black Mass by two women standing behind him.

Jeam Paul climbed aboard the open bed of the cart
and scrambled into the barrel.

This black Mass that had taken place the day before, involved a naked whore who was placed supinely on the high altar of Notre Dame Cathedral where the mock Mass was enacted upon her body. It also involved the sacrilegious burning of saint's relics. The incomprehensible burning of the disinterred bones of Saint Genevieve, the patron saint of the city of Paris could only be understood by a satanic cultist. The bones were sacrilegiously burned after the black Mass on the square in front of the Cathedral.

This was not Jean Paul's France. These were not his people. By some accident or purpose of the devil, he had been placed in a portal to hell to watch but not to enter.

As the gloominess deepened into dusk, one thought reverberated through his mind, he must get back to the Bocage to find General Castelineau. But first he would rest awhile.

≪

John Paul was not traveling south toward the Bocage,
but West to the sea!

CHAPTER 4

It was the rumbling of the cart's wheels on the Belgian block pavement that first awakened him. Dawn was breaking and the sun was flashing through the barrel cracks. Jean Paul pushed the lid of the barrel slightly aside and peered out. The cart was driven by a hunchback Breton and was full of snoring fishermen. Jean Paul was not traveling south toward the Bocage, but West to the sea!

He had been traveling for a dozen hours and his stomach was grumbling with hunger. He must take leave of his fish cart barrel and find some food, all without waking the snoring cargo. Slowly he lifted himself out of the barrel and slid down the side of the cart. He landed right into the waiting branches of an evergreen bush.

It scared him somewhat, but it did soften his fall from the cart. He need not have been so careful as the sleepers were slowly stretching, yawning and generally shaking themselves into mobility. Looking down the road, Jean Paul knew why. A two-story stone Inn was belching black smoke from its fore and aft chimneys.

As he approached the Inn, he noticed some cooks were astir in the place and his spirit bucked up at the prospect of a warm breakfast.

The fire in the middle of the Inn's great wall struck the chill from the room but provided only minimal light. In spite of the gloom, Jean Paul recognized a familiar face across the room.

"Henri, Henri!" Jean Paul shouted.

A trim, lanky man turned a weather-beaten face toward the shouting speaker. He bestirred himself from the table.

"It's me, Jean Paul, your brother!" announced Jean Paul.

The tall man said a few words to his companions and arising from his seat, placed a finger across his lips and made his way toward his younger brother.

"Not so loud. You're in a public place. The walls have ears." He whispered clasping his brother's shoulder in greeting.

"I've just left Paris. It was horrible!" exclaimed Jean Paul.

"General Castelineau sent me there. How goes the uprising?" he questioned stumbling over his words.

"Jean, Jean, let's get a table near the wall. I have much to tell you," returned his older brother.

Henri flagged a sleepy waiter, ordered two breakfasts and something hot to drink. "Let's wait a moment till he serves us before we begin. I trust no one. Show no emotion no matter what I tell you," cautioned Henri tapping Jean Paul's hand.

"First, General Castelineau is dead, shot through the head while leading a charge at Nantes. The other generals are disbursed throughout the Bocage.

Robespierre has sent one of France's finest regiments to the Vendee and they are wiping out the Vendeans. The scythes and shotguns are no match for the Regulars and their cannons."

Cupping his hands around his drink, Henri continued, "And now for the worst part, the Revolutionary army swept through the Bocage and took as prisoners all the relatives and sympathizers of the uprising…including our dear mother. She and three thousand others were marched to Nantes. You know how painful her legs are. In Nantes, they were put onto barges, hands tied behind their backs and taken to the middle of the Loire River where the barges were scuttled. With their hands tied…well…all were drowned. All that is left of our family, the DeBrosse family, is you and me."

Jean Paul stared at his brother slack-jawed in disbelief. His world was crumbling before his eyes. He prayed a short, fervent prayer for his mother.

"I barely got away with my life," whispered Henri, "I've joined a band of sailors. They have word that privateers are sailing from the coastal villages of Le Havre and Honfleur in a few weeks. They have all lost their families in this carnage. We intend to join the privateer's crew. If you are for it, I'll see if I can get you a berth," added Henri.

Jean Paul was still reeling from the shocking news that Henri had brought. He was trying to sort out the implications of each tragedy.

With his mother death and General Castelineau gone, the uprising in shambles, what was left of his life? Indeed, with Robespierre very much alive and the Revolution too, what was left of France?

Without thinking anymore, he stared intently at his brother and nodded yes. He would join the émigrés and become a corsair, a French privateer.

With six companions including his brother, they set out walking to Honfleur. Time passed quickly as Henri, the best talker in the group, easily regaled the company with his sea stories.

"When I left home in '88, you were just a babe, Jean Paul; I went straight to La Rochelle and joined what I thought was a fleet of small fishing smacks headed toward the channel."

All but Jean Paul broke out in laughter.

"I'm serious," Henri insisted, "Though I did think it queer that we left port at dusk instead of dawn."

The motley group of friends continued their laughter. Jean Paul turned to look at his shipmates to see if he could get an inkling as to what was so funny about his brother's statements.

"What I didn't know was that I had enlisted as a corsair! I thought we were going out to fish because most of the other boats were fishing," Henri continued in between gales of laughter, "But from that point on, I found pirating to be a tad more lucrative than fishing!"

As the group continued their amusement, Jean Paul began to fit the pieces of his childhood together. For years, his mother had mysteriously managed to find small amounts of money whenever she needed it and now Jean Paul understood how this was possible.

He began to look at his older brother with new eyes.

Pirating, for the common folk, was not considered a sin, not even an indiscretion, especially if you were not caught.

Henri had been caught only once by the British, but easily bought his way out of Folkstone jail after five months of hard labor.

Louis XVI himself had signed the fleet captain's *letters de marque* and as long as the countries whose ships that were raided were at war with France, it was considered legal to raid them. Pirates were not known to dot every 'i' and cross every 't', especially when they were hard at work at sea. In fact, many pirates found that they could cross over and back again between law and piracy with impunity.

This was not the only story Henri told. To Jean Paul's surprise, Henri had lived a very colorful life and now that he was considered a comrade, Jean Paul became privy to Henri's vivacious lifestyle.

One tale lead to another until the clutch of sailors found themselves in sight of the seaside town of Honfleur.

Henri led the group along the quay as he tried to spy one or two of the fishing smacks he had once sailed. Most of their eyes, however, caught sight of the massive tall masts atop the French ships berthed in the harbor of La Havre, across the bay on a spit of land on the north shore of the Seine river.

The British Channel fleet had bottled them up so that they could not escape beyond the mouth of the Seine River. The officers of the French fleet were all ashore or at home drawing only half pay until word came that the embargo had been lifted or breached.

To the practiced eye of a seaman even the bare riggings and the masts gave away the name of the ships. So with the help of Henri's spyglass, liberated from the British on one of his cross-channel raids, the group was sure they could make out the masts, spars, and halyards of a half dozen Man-of-War frigates, even with the identifying sails all furled.

There were six frigates: *Le Bussole*, *Le Boideeose*, the *Dauphin Royal*, with her sister ship, the *Le Soleil Royal*, the *Le Reserche* and the *Charles*. Then, they spotted a corvette, a small naval scout ship, named *Le Romance*. Although she carried a dozen twelve pounders, the British sneered at her non-naval name but they shouldn't have, for they, too, sailed a similar vessel with the non-fighting name of *My True Love*.

Most of the ships carried seventy-four guns and thus in the French Navy they were entitled to be called first-rate warships. The British, however, tended to give the term first-rate to ships bearing over one hundred guns.

Absorbed as they were with identifying the ships in the Le Havre harbor, across the bay, the group had failed to notice that they had wandered a fair distance along the wharf to where there was less traffic. There they spotted the Anatole, a French lugger, and while she was no paragon of French naval warfare, she was indigenous to the French coast.

The Anatole was built as a coastal fishing boat and only later was converted into a vessel of war. Seventy feet long with an eighteen foot beam she could, with her eight foot draft, abandon the ocean and run up the mouth of almost any river that emptied into the sea.

Very few British ships could follow the lugger up river.

She had only one deck but it covered a spacious hold. Her long slender hull and her rakish mizzenmast and spanker sails, hung far over her stern, giving her speed and maneuverability that was only matched by the quite smaller, swift corvette boats.

She had the look of a slaver ship and like a slaver her fish or slave cargo had to reach land fast.

But with all of this speed, she had no beauty to her at all. To her crew she was just a work boat. Her plainness served Henri and Jean Paul just fine and they intended that to work to their advantage. They boarded the Anatole and joined the crew of forty men.

Jean Paul's job on board the boat, along with five other

young men, mostly pre teen-age boys, was to go below deck, receive leather bags filled with a pint of highly explosive gun powder from the gunner who made up the magazine charges. Between the powder monkey and the gunner hung wet curtains made from strips of cotton. The moist curtain kept any stray sparks from reaching the powder magazine. The powder monkey would carry the gunpowder to the gun crew. It was considered a most dangerous job, for a lad of tender years, for if one spark would stray, the entire ship could blow up.

Before a battle, the pyramid of cannon shots was taken apart and each shot was placed securely in a length of board with round holes in it to hold the shots from rolling across the deck. The cannons on the Anatole were round and fat. The gunners used turkey quills filled with small amounts of gunpowder as a lighter and fired their twelve pound shots upwards, looping them high into the air and letting them drop on the enemy's deck, much like mortar fire. This kind of fire was a crew killer. When the shot was exploding with canisters of rifle balls, they wreaked havoc on the enemy crew. This idea was not to sink the enemy ship, (ships were too valuable as a war prize), but to kill or disable the crew, making the vessel capture a certainty.

It was on that moonless night with a soft windward breeze blowing down channel, that the skipper of the Anatole, Captain Marchand, chose to slip the hawsers of the Anatole's anchor and quietly glide past the mouth of the Seine River.

"Look-outs aloft," the Captain commanded. "The hounds be out tonight!"

He was referring to the two frigates that King George III had specifically designated to capture or sink the Anatole. In fact, the two hounds, one named the HMS Greyhound; the faster chaser vessel, and the other the HMS Wolfhound; the slower killer vessel, were on detached service from the Channel Fleet with orders to capture and hang Captain Marchand without trial.

Marchand had worried the British command for better than six months, sinking two of their corvettes and badly damaging a frigate; all besides ravaging the British coast.

The Anatole was but ten miles down the coast when a British fog rolled over the sea. Fog on the sea is cursed anytime by sailors, but especially so in a sea battle.

With ships moving in and out of fog banks and cloud cover, a gray goose on a sunless sea was easier to distinguish than a friend or foe frigate on the prowl. Because a cannon's reach was quite short, around 100 yards, a gunner would often refuse to fire at a gray ghost slipping through the changing sea. His hesitation was often perilous.

In a whisper heard less than ten yards away, a topman on the fighting top cupped his hand to his mouth,

"Two points abaft the starboard beam, a hound. I see a hound."

Without a sound, the chase was on. As the Anatole's helmsman pushed the helm hard alee, the pirate vessel silently swung away from the British frigate.

"I wonder if she saw us," exclaimed a gunner.

"No matter," responded a Lieutenant, "Seeing is not engaging."

"Powder monkey, tell the portside gunner's mate to load all port guns," bellowed Captain Marchand.

"Quartermaster, make a mile loop around the stern of that there British Greyhound. Stay behind her wake and run parallel to her. Take care not to rob her sails of wind, at least not yet. And mind her stern chasers when you round her galleries," he added.

He was referring to the two cannons that protected the rear of the frigate. Seldom used because most battles were fought broadside to broadside, these cannons, nevertheless, did chase away any warships that could follow them.

"We've got the jump on her," grinned Henri as he slapped Jean Paul's backside, "Get them cannons loaded."

Jean Paul was already moving down the gangway to draw powder pouches. "This is going to be exciting," he murmured to himself.

The lugger had now moved past the HMS Greyhound and rounded her stern. Jean Paul could now see the tactic they were going to use. Only a foggy night would make this ploy work. The Greyhound might smell the lugger but she could not see her through the fog.

Most sea battles were fought broadside to broadside.

Smiling as he worked, Jean Paul saw to it that all the guns he was charged with serving were loaded and ready. He even checked the work of the other powder monkeys on the port aft while supplying turkey quills filled with powder to the gunners.

He was so excited that he failed to notice that the lugger had slowed down almost to a stop. The wind had failed and now the Greyhound was making full use of its canvases and was slipping away.

A silent prayer fell from Jean Paul's lips, "Oh God, don't let them get away."

No sooner had he finished than the capricious wind picked up again filling the bunting of the lugger's sails while sucking the wind from the Greyhounds sails. The race was on again.

Jean Paul could see clearly that they were racing with the wind. They were the wind!

"On my command," began Captain Marchand, "with double canisters loaded. Raking, fire, commence."

Jean Paul could not believe it. He was about to engage in his first sea combat.

The maneuver had taken the British quite by surprise. Their eyes, their vessel, their whole attention was directed forward. An attack from the rear was unheard of.

The rear facing 32 pounder stern chasers were still lashed in travel position, it would take some time to unleash and load them.

As each gun of the Anatole passed the poop deck of the Greyhound, it fired, raking the quarterdeck, main deck, and forecastle from starboard to portside leaving a devastating path of shattered timbers, torn rope, wounded and dead men in its wake.

Engaging in combat at sea.

The attack lasted but fifteen minutes, but it effectively destroyed the Greyhound's combat effectiveness. When the violence of the attack subsided, the lugger had sailed past the reach of the British guns. Captain Marchand did not reengage the Greyhound, but set a course for St. Malo, further south on the French coast.

He was well aware that his luck was running out and if the British frigate caught up with him, her 32 pounders would crush him instantly. The distance the Anatole needed to travel was substantial. From what Captain Marchand determined they were off the coast of St. Mere-Eglise. He held course well off the shallow shores that had grounded more than one inattentive helmsman.

"If we can make it down the coast, we can surely lose the British," whispered Henri to his brother.

Though he knew not the location of the Cape his brother spoke of, Jean Paul still nervously nodded in agreement.

"They won't follow us this close to the mainland," finished Henri.

As they rounded the city of Audenville, a leeward wind caught their sails forcing them to reset them for a starboard tack.

"Better get below, we're going to make a run for it," shouted Henri, "This wind will blow the fog away and then we'll be fair game."

Henri could not have been more right except that the danger was not behind them, but in front of them.

They were sailing right into a trap set by the two British Hounds. This time it was the Wolfhound's turn. Though no one on board the Anatole could see it through the pitch blackness of early morn, the teeth of the Wolfhound were ready.

As Jean Paul stopped by the gangway to the lower deck he glanced skyward and saw a most unusual sight.

Six evenly spaced stars were dancing high in the pre-dawn sky.

The odd thing was that they were orange in color and grew in size and brightness. In a second, Jean Paul's ears went deaf and most of those six stars exploded simultaneously below the Anatole's deck.

The horrific noise was the last sensation that Jean Paul felt. He was immediately catapulted into the water, unaware of his wetness. He knew he must be dead or dying, when suddenly another louder explosion shook his eardrums.

One of those stars must have reached the powder magazine of the Anatole.

She was no more. Wood, ropes, canvases, sailor bodies were all floating together in a watery mass of flotsam. He remembered grabbing a timber before falling unconscious.

✍

"Suddenly another louder explosion shook his eardrums..."

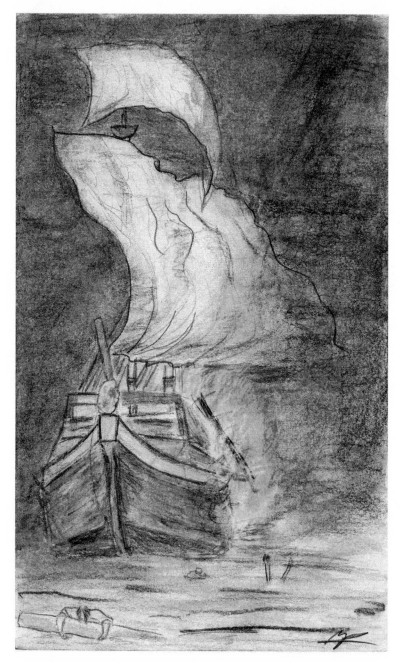

Wood, canvases, sailor bodies were all floating together...

CHAPTER 5

It seemed like hours, even days to Jean Paul's befogged mind. The first of his feelings to reassert itself was his abiding sense of deep penetrating cold, bone chilling cold.

Deep within Jean Paul's memory he remembered Brother Benoit's description of hell. Hell was not hot, but bitter cold. Brother Benoit was right, he thought. The Italian writer, Dante, had told of hell being cold…very cold. This certainly was where Jean Paul was and the mere thought of this frigid hell made him struggle to climb up higher on the log.

He felt a thump as he bumped into something solid. Next, he felt a warm hand reaching for him, pulling at his nearly frozen body. He heard what sounded to him like, "Umgalase." It meant nothing at the time but when he opened his eyes he saw what surely was a devil crawling in the chains below the channel of a boat not a yard above the sea.

It was lunging for him desperately trying to grab him from his watery grave.

When Jean Paul's eyes cleared a bit from the salt water, he could make out a huge figure of a man whose body and arms were covered with black designs of indescribable meanings. Surely he was in hell and this devil was grabbing for him, for his soul. Jean Paul was too weak to resist. The devil could take him.

"Coquelin," shouted a deep French voice, "I've got his arm, you get his butt. I think this one is still alive."

A silly thought flashed through Jean Paul's mind, So Frenchmen went to hell?"

The man named Coquelin lifted Jean Paul up over the deck rail and into the arms of a fellow mariner. When a blanket was placed over him, Jean Paul fell back into a deep sleep.

"Well, he's your fish, Coquelin. You caught him." A fading voice said.

Jean Paul was glad that he was caught. Hell or no Hell.

Dawn broke bright and clear as the black sails of the ship, *Diablo Dauphin*, entered the harbor of St. Malo, a few leagues south from the area of Anatole's demise.

Captain Robert Moulin-Bleu was very disappointed. Although they saved some fellow pirates, the evening's adventure was a total loss for his him, his king, and the Archbishop of St. Malo under whose flag he sailed. Economically it was a disaster.

St. Malo, an island a short distance from the French shore, was a curious mix of church-state relations, founded by saints Aaron and Brendan.

Although early Roman evidence appeared to pre-date the church's early findings in the sixth century, the city's true beginning began with St. Malo, a disciple of St. Brendan, who took up residence on the island in the early 500's during the first millennium.

Eventually, a causeway between the city island and the shore was filled in, making St. Malo a permanent attachment to

Jean Paul felt a warm hand reaching for him,
pulling at his nearly frozen body...

the French coast.

In the middle of the 12th century a bishop named Jean de Chatillon, capitalized on the city's great desire for independence from the French government by granting right of asylum to all people of France who were suspected of committing a crime. No one could be tried for a crime after simply entering the gates of St. Malo. This action drew, of course, every felon, petty criminal, thief, or would-be thief into St. Malo.

The stipend for this ecclesiastical favor was, of course, a percentage of gains gotten by these new residents paid to the mayor, the king, and the bishop. This right applied to corsairs, pirates, and other wolves of the sea as well.

Robert Surcouf, a well-known ship builder by trade, immediately enlarged his business by adding corsairing to his craft. St. Malo's fame, wealth, and respect were now launched.

When the black-sailed brigantine settled into her dock and the heavy landlines were secured, Jean Paul opened his eyes and looked around.

He saw the back of the tall, lean, and tattooed Indian who had plucked him from the sea talking in animated French to a laughing collection of his compatriots. Jean Paul saw the furled sails above him, smelled the smoke pouring out of the cook's shack behind him and two dogs vying with each other to lick the salt water from his face.

He groaned once catching his breath and the group of sailors turned toward him.

"Look, Coquelin," said one sailor pointing to the boy, "he's awake!"

"Get him some soup, Coquelin," said another.

A bull whip whistled then cracked in the air above Jean Paul.

"Don't feed this dog or he will never leave. Dump him on shore. He'll find his way," growled the captain.

Coquelin stood up to his full six foot three inch height.

"I caught him...he's mine...he stays," and then in a lowered voice, "or we both go."

The last statement stopped Captain Moulin-Bleu in full anger. He had lost his navigator on the last long trip. He could not afford to lose the best topman he had ever known in Coquelin now.

"We'll settle this tonight," replied the Captain turning on his heels and heading for the quarter deck.

Coquelin knew the mettle of the Captain and the mood of the crew. They both could turn on him and his young 'fish'.

Mohawk Indian, Coquelin.

So as soon as the crew left for shore, Coquelin took the young lad into the navigator's cabin, located across the passageway from the quartermaster's cabin. Both cabins were on the quarterdeck behind the helm, but it provided enough privacy for Coquelin to talk.

Once inside the navigator's cabin, Coquelin cast the full force of his stare onto Jean Paul, and with the most serious deep voice, spoke, "Besides powder monkey, do you know how sail ship?"

Even with Coquelin encouraging stare, Jean Paul could only answer, "No."

"That bad," replied Coquelin. "Aboard corsair we elect crew. If crew not like you or you not work boat, you leave. Be thankful we in port!"

Jean Paul's nervous eyes roamed the cabin. He searched every corner and niche looking for a clue, something to save himself from any more disaster.

Then he spotted it. There it was, at the back of the navigator's desk; a full six volume set of Bezout's Art and Practice of Navigation. It was a geographic history of all the oceans and seas of the world.

It showed the winds, tides, headlands, beaches, sea features, islands and land masses known. Almost every navigator mariner had one. Brother Benoit had taught the course at his school in the Vendee.

Like a thunderclap, it hit him. He could navigate! Most sailors, including new captains, could not.

Jean Paul flashed a smile as his eyes met Coquelin and Coquelin smiled back at this new navigator he had fished from the sea and saved from certain death.

It was almost midnight when the crew of the *Diablo Dauphin* returned from shore leave. They were glum, dispirited, and angry. They knew the meeting that Captain Robert Moulin-Bleu called would be very important.

This was no meeting to divide plunder, but possibly one to elect a new captain, especially if he called for a vote to reject Coquelin's new friend. A crew without Coquelin would be sad indeed.

The meeting would be held below deck.

Coquelin and Jean Paul would be detained under guard on the forecastle deck until called for. Coquelin was the first to be summoned below.

The pirate ship, *Diablo Dauphin.*

The cavernous ward room easily held half a hundred mariners loitering, sitting, and laying in all kinds of positions.

All of this was completely understandable to Coquelin who, coming from his Mohawk tribe remembered that the Indians always held a general council meeting whenever any matter of great importance was to be undertaken by the tribe. All adults in the tribe were entitled to vote including women. There was no particular leader of the discussion but every man had the ability to interject his thoughts and then at a certain point they would all be called upon to vote.

Unlike the English, Spanish and other European nations, the Indian tribes did not adhere to one-man-one-rule. The chief of the tribe might be their leader for battle, for hunting, for selecting where they were to live or camp, but others might occupy those functions as well. To be a spokesman for the tribe might be the chief's primary job but anyone could undertake to be the spokesman as well.

As a result, the Indian tribes had a very democratic society. This was not understandable at all to the European nations who tried to work with them, but the similarity between the Indian tribe's governance and the governance of the pirates fitted right in with Coquelin's understanding of freedom.

Try as he might, Jean Paul could only make out muffled talk punctuated by slammed fists and curse words. The Captain tried to keep a semblance of order but the arguments would boil over again.

"The only question then to be settled is what percentage of loot we give to this man charged with such a responsible job?" yelled the Captain.

Voices ebbed and flowed with 'yea's and 'nay's following each discourse until finally after much lively discussion the

crew settled upon an eighth of the prize be awarded to the new navigator from the booty procured.

At last, one man dressed in cut-off pants and stocking cap staggered up the gangway beckoning Jean Paul below. Jean Paul could make out just three candles illuminating the cabin. He recognized the hulk of Coquelin in the corner of the room and watched him carefully as he entered the room.

"The question comes down to this," opened the Captain addressing Jean Paul, "Can you navigate this vessel night or day, storm or clear? If you can, we can use you; our old navigator was washed overboard."

Jean Paul began to equivocate a mumbled answer.

"I know you found Bezout's volumes and that you can read," prompted the Captain noticing Jean Paul's hesitation.

Then in a loud clear voice, Jean Paul responded,

"I know how to read the celestial bodies. I know how to navigate using a Sextant and Chronometer, assuming those instruments have been well cared for and precise." He shot a look back at the Captain.

"With a Back Staff, on a sunny afternoon, I can gauge the horizon and with your Octant and some luck, I can calculate our latitude using the bright stars or the sun and the horizon."

Jean Paul scanned his stunned audience and felt more and more confident as he continued,

"I can also read a log-line to determine your vessels' speed. I have a fundamental knowledge of all land masses and have used a map before. I know how to figure latitude and am a little familiar with the new ways to find longitude, especially if you've got a good, reliable clock. I know the points on a compass rose; the dangers of a riptide and the signs of a shallowing beach."

Jean Paul finished his litany of talents and looked around the room for a response and when he heard none, he added,

"I'm a scant coastal sailor. I know more ships are lost near the shore than ever lost on the main."

The room was silent. Coquelin's head barely moved with a small nod, he knew that Jean Paul would be hired.

Finally, the Captain banged his fist on the table and eyed each man, jack-of-them.

"Well, that's it then. You hold our brains afloat, and until you run us aground we're in your hands. Well mates, break out the grog then. We have a new navigator, Jean Paul,

To determine a ship's location on the ocean,
navigators used a time piece, called a chronometer, and an
instrument to measure the angle of the sun and the horizon,
called an octant, later replaced
by the more accurate sextant.

first mate to the quartermaster and with like privileges. Any questions?? Then proceed to load provisions for tomorrow."

Jean Paul's navigator position was however, not a secure lifetime, irrevocable position. Should he fail or make a major mistake his removal would be swift, decisive and fatal by quickly removing him overboard, at which point the crew would hold another council and elect another navigator. This was a veritable threat to all on board a pirate ship; anyone could be reduced to a non-entity by a simple vote of a majority of the crew.

As a parting shot Captain Robert Moulin-Bleu patted Coquelin on his shoulder,

"Give our new fish a tour of the *Diablo* tomorrow. Show him the fore'top gallants. We'll give him his sea legs yet!"

Now that the business of the navigation was finished, the entire crew relaxed and the rum began to flow. Captain Moulin-Bleu tapped the rum keg while watching the crew drink themselves into a stupor. He was content with the knowledge that by dawn the rum would be gone, the crew fast asleep and he would once again be secure in his command.

When dawn suddenly burst over the furled sails, Coquelin was already up and vigorously waking Jean Paul into consciousness. Coquelin rarely drank and therefore was always posted to the dawn watch. A job which he liked and the crew was glad he did. Being the first awake he had the distinct duty and joy of firing the morning gun, a small swivel deck gun mounted on the railing of the poop deck. It alerted everyone on board that the day at sea had begun. When sailing in convoy, it awakened the entire fleet. He loved this British naval custom.

Coquelin shouted in his broken French, "Time to show you boat!"

A groggy-eyed Jean Paul staggered to his feet and

followed Coquelin to the poop deck at the rear of the vessel.

"*Diablo*," Coquelin continued motioning to the ship, "ninety feet six long, twenty four feet six wide, eleven feet deep. Helm, on quarter deck below, outside your cabin. Captain quarters down gangway from you. Captain keep eye on you, all times."

Nodding his head in the direction of the front of the ship, Coquelin continued, "Most crew sleep in fo'castle."

Coquelin grinned from ear to ear. "I tall, I sleep any place."

Then pointing skyward to the highest sails, he continued, "I spend most time work up there. I called topman. Too dangerous for most. You fall from top, no search. You dead! I take you up soon."

Coquelin, still smiling began to explain the workings of the ship, "To make ship go fast, spread three jibs, lift bow of ship out of water, drive ship forward, make speed. Bowsprit in front of ship is long, pointy… it hold sails, tied to bowsprit, large waves make dangerous work in bad weather to work on it."

Jean Paul tried to keep up with Coquelin as he walked swiftly to the front of the ship and looked up to the main sails, "Behind tall main mast is big sails, main push for boat, use for power. On back of main mast is gaff-rigged sail, give boat steering. Come now, I take you up foremast. You see far from there."

Jean Paul was wide-eyed and awake now; trying to soak in all the information, while Coquelin was completely at ease and in his element.

Waving his hands and fingers, Coquelin continued, "Come, over to foremast ratline. I stand behind you, steady your climb. You must climb ratline with wind at back, or you be blown into sea."

Very carefully, Jean Paul placed his feet in the tarred holes of the rope ladder called a ratline. Coquelin pushed him from behind until both of them reached the first fighting top platform twenty feet above the deck.

Coquelin shouted, "Go through landlubber hole and climb up next ratline."

As Jean Paul struggled to focus on the small hole in the fighting top platform, he suddenly realized that Coquelin was no longer behind him. To his amazement he saw that Coquelin was on the main shroud above him and was pulling himself upward. Jean Paul froze in his tracks as he watched Coquelin vault upward through several layers of ropes, sails and yards until he had reached the very top of the main mast.

Jean Paul knew that something spectacular was about to happen.

Placing his belt across the top mast main shroud, Coquelin slid down to the fore gallant backstay, caught his balance at the foretop and then reversed his direction. He bounced against the now billowing bunt of the sail sliding down the main shroud and then neatly placed his rump on the foredeck of the captain's gig mounted in the middle of the ship's deck.

The crew which had been loading supplies had stopped to watch this brilliant display of courage and agility and broke into cheers and hurrahs.

In spite of Coquelin's enthusiastic beckoning, Jean Paul remained glued to his ratline until the cheers ended and then very slowly and clumsily began his descent down to the deck. When his feet hit the deck, Jean Paul ran over to Coquelin and

Sailors climbing on ship's rigging.

pummeled him with congratulatory jabs in his arm. He could not believe the performance that he had just witnessed. He would have to speak to this man and learn some of his secrets for he was mightier than any man Jean Paul had ever known.

That afternoon the crew was loading the vessel with food, clothing, gunpowder, weapons, and curiously, trade goods. They were off on another cruise much longer than the first outing, but because of the rank that Coquelin and Jean Paul enjoyed they were excused from the heavy duty of loading the vessel. So, Jean Paul took Coquelin back to his room on the quarterdeck and began to question him on what he had just witnessed. Coquelin smiled. He knew it was a long story, but he would abbreviate it for his new friend.

"I born Canada near Mont-real. I, Mohawk, Iroquois," Coquelin began, "My people are tribe with no fear, work at great height. No fear of it. To us, working high is gift from gods. No white man can do."

Coquelin held his closed fist to his heart as he spoke, watching Jean Paul slowly comprehend his story.

Jean Paul then knew that was why Coquelin could handle the very high sail work done by a topman on sailing ships. Coquelin had no apprehension working far above the ground. Most men would get to the footrope and inch their way across the yard to do their work from that level, but Coquelin could run up the ratlines all the way to the main yards, dart across the top of them and then slide down the footrope to be in position to furl or unfurl the sails as needed.

Coquelin's tribe came from Canada and so, in a sense, he was trained in Mohawk, French, English and Ojibwa. But Coquelin was unique; he held the best characteristics of all those nations. Somewhere in his background, the Jesuit fathers who had come from France had taught him something of religion but it was such that he never gave up his belief in the Great Spirit.

As a child in Canada during the summer, Coquelin would wander the forests near his home observing the British cutting the Royal blaze mark on the tall trees near the shore which the British used as replacement masts for their ships that had lost their masts in storms or other ill adventures. The British grew their own masts in the new world and blazed them with a special mark which told all

"Do not touch this tree. It belongs to the King of England."

It was his love of the forest and trees which first attracted Coquelin to the ocean, for he would wander through the forests spying on the English blazed trees, climbing high in them. At one point, he saw in the harbor below large sailing ships that sported those great timbers he had once climbed. He had to go see them and when he was older he gained the courage to go down to the shore, meet and befriend some of the seamen and finally board one of the great ships.

It was a British ship he had boarded and they so admired Coquelin's ability to mount the masts and run along the yards that they gave him a job right on the spot. Armed with that freedom, Coquelin sailed north with the British all the way to Halifax, Nova Scotia where his love affair with the British Union Jack ended.

◅

WILD IS THE WIND - RICHARD LOUIS FEDERER

CHAPTER 6

By noon, the ship was three quarters loaded and the crew of the *Diablo Dauphin* was getting anxious about where they were going. Captain Robert Moulin-Bleu had not yet arrived but the quartermaster, Charles Bateaux had, carrying an arm full of maps, sextants, chronometers and some compasses.

"Ahoy, navigator! How about a hand!" yelled Bateaux.

Jean Paul jumped to his feet to help the new arrival.

"Most of this stuff is for you," continued Bateaux, "I'll settle for two compasses and a pair of lanterns. The rest is yours."

Then seeing Coquelin he questioned, "You showed him the *Diablo*?"

Coquelin smiled in reply.

"Did you show him your basket weave back? You know the checkered weave shirt?"

Coquelin's lips tightened as the smile left his face.

"Here, Jean Paul, take a look."

Bateaux flipped the back of Coquelin's shirt revealing a scarred, beaten and scourged backside. Indeed his skin looks like a piece of old shredded meat. Coquelin had once been beaten by two boatswain mates, one on each side of his back causing the basket weave scars that would be there forever.

Jean Paul was shocked. Not only by the absolute cruelty of the beating but by the unflinching courage of a man who could receive it and not die from the shear pain of it.

"How?" was the only word that escaped Jean Paul's lips.

"How indeed," agreed the quartermaster. Do you tell him or do I?"

Coquelin did not answer but with his head down he briskly bumped his way out of their company.

"It happened two, maybe three years ago when Coquelin left Mont-real. He is a Mohawk from the Algonquin tribe...not afraid of heights, you know," started Bateaux.

Jean Paul nodded.

"Well, one day while searching for British blazed masts, he espied a British man-of-war at anchor in a cove near his home. He saw those tall masts and wanted to climb them and so he visited the ship which had come from Nova Scotia with English troops bound for New England. The officers showed him aboard and watched him climb the rigging. Have you seen him do the same aboard this ship?"

Jean Paul nodded again.

"They immediately impressed him into the British Navy and sailed to Nova Scotia. Well, off the coast of Halifax, a mighty gale blew up with lightening, some ice and the full force of the wind. No man wanted to go aloft to furl the top gallant sails with Coquelin.

He begged the young officer in charge of the detail for just one more topman to help him furl the sail. None would volunteer, so Coquelin who spoke little English refused to go it alone. The young boatswain officer began to beat Coquelin with his wicker stick. Amidst the storm, hail and ice Coquelin begged him to stop beating him and help him round up some more help, all to no avail.

When the wicker lash stung across Coquelin's lips and mouth, he could no longer hold his anger. Grabbing a capstan bar, he crushed it against the young officer's cheek, ear and head. The result was immediate as the officer fell to the deck, while others came to subdue the enraged Indian. Coquelin was seen smashing the sailor and officers alike, including the Captain's executive officer, Josua Fitt, Second in Command. Coquelin was immediately chained to the deck in leg irons to ride out the storm in his semi-nakedness.

To make matters worse the inexperienced officer was the nephew of the Captain, and when the Captain saw his injuries, he knew that the young boatswain's naval career was over. The Captain knew he would have to explain to his sister why he did not intervene, and why he allowed his young apprentice to act so rashly. The details of that evening would have to be put into words that would shift the blame to Coquelin. His nephew would not be the one put on trial.

A trial was set for the next day and since Coquelin was not a regular British sailor, the incident was not entered in the man-of-war's log book. The trial was a farce; Coquelin was guilty of battering an officer. The punishment for which was so severe that the entire Navy present would remember that transgression forever. Though death was demanded, a less severe punishment would accomplish the same end, flogging throughout the fleet. There were twelve war ships lying at anchor in the harbor of Halifax, Nova Scotia and at twenty lashings per boat that would be 240 stripes on the naked flesh. Even with a doctor riding in the whipping boat no sailor could ever survive such a beating.

The following day, the davits of the man-of-war lowered a draft boat with eight oarsmen, one marine guard and a coxswain to steer the boat. A second boat was then lowered containing one marine guard, the ships medical doctor and one coxswain to steer the punishment boat which was tethered to the draft boat. In the center of the punishment boat stood the condemned Coquelin lashed between two capstan bars, the bottoms of which were spread athwart at the beam of the boat. On either side of Coquelin, stood two of the fleet's best boatswains holding whips, called cattails.

First, one and then the other would forcefully lay their whips on his condemned body in alternative stripes which etched the blood basket weave marks on his back. Twenty stripes per ship and each whipping was laid on the flesh by the eager arms of new warships boatswain mates.

The morning sun arose dull and red, a danger sign known to all sailors. Coquelin stepped on board the punishment boat, made room for the now almost drunken surgeon who had been nipping at the rum bottle since breakfast. The rum was for the prisoner, not the doctor but the doctor knew that the prisoner would be dead before the bottle was empty.

Coquelin made no sound when the first pair of lashes did their work. At the second beating tears ran from his eyes as he winced at the blows.

Coquelin was offered the bottle but informed the doctor that Indians did not drink.

The tethered ships were becoming more difficult to manage just as the puffy white clouds had become angry and black from the approaching storm rolling their way.

The boats were bobbing like corks and though Coquelin could still stand, his punishers could not.

As the tethered boats made their way to the third vessel one of the new boatswain fell overboard and as he tried to clamber aboard, the lieutenant in charge became more nervous. The sea was now much too violent to continue the punishment. It was time to postpone the flogging to a calmer day. The navy manuals provided for this eventuality.

On the way back to the first man-of-war, Coquelin's boat suddenly capsized catapulting everyone into the waters. Realizing his escape was suddenly at hand, Coquelin dived into the deep. His hands were unburdened by the ropes which were now loosened. He swam underwater with all of his might toward the shore with the storm at its heights; he remained unseen by the crew and their officers.

A half-hour's swim put him on the beach of an island covered with oak trees. Coquelin dragged himself into the nearby woods.

The next morning he searched the small island on which he had landed. By noon he had discovered several ruffians loading a small boat on the leeward side of the island. Making their acquaintance he soon found a berth on a black-sailed brigantine ship heading for the South American coast.

And that Mr. Navigator is why your friend Coquelin hates the British and will never sail under the Union Jack flag again. He still owes them two hundred blows worth of beatings and the British never forget."

At that moment Coquelin reentered the cabin, "Captain want you, Jean Paul."

Without hesitating, Jean Paul flew down the gangway and wrapped his fingers on the Captain's cabin door.

"Come in," blurted the captain, "Jean Paul, we leave with the dawn tide. Set a course for the Azores as soon as we clear the harbor. I must meet the Bishop. He has just returned from Paris. I'll return late tonight. "

"Very well," replied Jean Paul, "We will be ready to sail with the tide."

Jean Paul returned to his cabin to review his maps before Captain Moulin-Bleu returned. The course to the Azores was not too difficult to plot. Once clear of the St. Malo waters, he would follow the French coastline to Bordeaux. Then at night, turn, following the latitude parallel due west and then drop down on the second meridian west of Bordeaux onto the Azores.

᷍

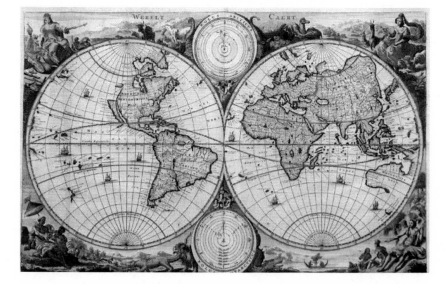

CHAPTER 7

The prison guards of the Revolution in Paris were not regular soldiers, but rather citizen volunteers caught up in the zeal of the revolutionary ardor. After a few weeks of military duty, boredom set in with the daily routine of guard duty. So, to make their life more interesting, the guards would accept small bribes from the prisoners for food, newspapers, clothing items and such. If there were any argument over the bribes, the guards always won out because every prisoner at Saint Sulpice would eventually lose their heads and no one had ever escaped. For those prisoners who could afford it, it made their remaining hours more bearable, and for the guards who accepted the bribes, it provided amusement while lining their pockets with small change.

So it was, that the guard Monsieur Duprey became friendly with, accepted ever larger bribes for ever larger favors. Monsieur DuPrey had three days to subvert his guard because on the fourth day the river coachman, Georges, would return from Versailles on his way up the Seine River, stopping at the city of Melun. He and his wife had to be on that river coach. Monsieur DuPrey's daughters would be anxiously waiting for them to be on board.

That constant thought of their beautiful daughters kept the DuPreys alive and hopeful throughout their dreadful ordeal.

Through the course of the week, Monsieur DuPrey and his wife had sold or traded all of their fine clothing and apparel reducing themselves to a collection of rags which made them look like the wretched poor of Paris. They managed to strategically hide their remaining gold coins from curious eyes so that they could use them when the time was right.

DuPrey had secured some bee's wax through his bartering, claiming it relieved his wife from the putrid odors that permeated the Saint Sulpice prison. That seemed to satisfy the guard who provided it, but DuPrey intended to use it for a much more significant purpose.

Executions occurred in the early morning hours, and so to make their escape, the DuPreys needed to formulate a plan quickly. The docket was determined by the Revolutionaries and given to the guards. It was pre-dawn when Monsieur DuPrey arranged, via a large gold bonus, to have their guard go to the Tennis Courts, where the Revolutionaries met, to find out when they were scheduled to stand trial.

Just as the guard was leaving their cell, however, DuPrey jammed the latch of the door with the bee's wax so that the door would not close properly. With most people still asleep, and the darkness cloaking their movements, they were able to escape unnoticed. With their heads hung low, the DuPrey's gathered buckets and mops near their cell door and followed three slop-bucket carriers out of the building and into the street.

Within fifteen minutes after leaving the prison walls, the pair was at the banks of the Seine, scanning up and down the river for some sign of their boat.

Most boats were dark as no one had risen for the morning

The DuPreys had to escape the Saint Sulpice prison,
or they would be executed.

yet, but just as dawn neared, Monsieur DuPrey caught sight of George's rivercoach with their night lamps burning to welcome them on onboard.

George had hired a draft horse to pull the cordell up river. Using a horse allowed the barge to travel twice as fast as a man pulling the rope, and speed was paramount for the success of the DuPrey escape. But, as the boat pulled away from the shores, Georges had one more duty to perform. The enthusiastic cries and laughter from the DuPrey girls were heard echoing off the banks of the river. Georges shushed the whole family into the belly of the barge. It was a happier trip back to Melun than their leaving had been.

Once clear of the outskirts of Paris, Georges lit the breakfast stove, and then called out to his nephew riding the draft horse on the shoreline to not stop for any passengers until they reached Melun.

Monsieur DuPrey caught sight of George's rivercoach with their night lamps burning to welcome them on onboard.

With the boat moving swiftly upstream, Georges was finally able to join in the conversation with the joyous family he had on board below.

"The boy who saved us," shouted out Angelique Marie, "How is he? Did you ever find him?"

"Well, I saw him splash into the Seine and swim to shore. I'm sure he escaped alright. He was heading toward Paris," replied Georges.

With a thoughtful glance toward his family DuPrey said, "He seemed like a respectable young man. Surely he will be saved."

Angelique looked at her sister, Claire, and then her mother, "Oh yes, yes. I'm sure he will be alright."

"He saved our lives. All of us," declared Monsieur DuPrey, "It will be my pleasure to meet him again someday."

Angelique Marie smiled again and replied, "I am certain

we will meet him again."

Madame DuPrey glanced knowingly toward her husband and finally stood up and said, "Come children, eat something."

The journey to the Motherhouse at Melun took two days. To say that Brother Marcuse was surprised at the arrival of his new guests was more than an understatement, it was a shock. Brother Marcuse would have to find suitable rooms, food and wine for them. He was used to housing men in the motherhouse, but having women under his roof was quite unorthodox, and it made him quite uneasy.

Monsieur DuPrey needed to return to his business and that required him to be away for nearly a month, but his family needed a hiding place during that time.

Sensing how uncomfortable Brother Marcuse was at having women around, he offered to have his wife and daughters cook and clean the monastery as payment for their housing.

Dawn on the Seine River in Paris

This would allow Brother Marcuse time to pursue other interests.

This freedom from daily chores seemed to lighten his mood and so an agreement was struck. The girls ran the monastery and Brother Marcuse tended the garden.

For the next few months, Angelique Marie and Claire discovered many hidden treasures in the extensive halls of the ancient edifice. They especially liked the huge library upstairs where they spent long hours reading.

During one of their explorations in the library they found class work and journals from prior students of the Christian Brother's school. One student in particular caught Angelique Marie's attention as she perused through the old coursework. She found the journals of a Vendean named, Jean Paul DeBrosse, and she was certain it was the same young man she met on the river.

Angelique Marie was quite intrigued by his thoughts and writings even if they were written when he was younger. After her daily chores, Angelique would run up to the library spending hours reading what Jean Paul had read, and learning what he had learned. This unlikely coincidence was to become the beginning of a understanding of the young man who saved her life.

๛

CHAPTER 8

The archipelago of nine islands and eight smaller islands called "ants" lay just 950 miles west of Lisbon. They were Portuguese owned and used by nations and pirates alike for resupplies and water. The islands were considered the most beautiful in the Atlantic, and from a distance their blue haze dubbed them azure.

The trip would take about 2 to 3 weeks at the most, thought Jean Paul. They would have to change their canvases to brown linen from nighttime pirate black, posing as traders so as not arouse suspicions.

"Thank God," Jean Paul thought, "This first trip would be easy."

With all of his work plotted Jean Paul could finally allow his mind to relax and to recall all that had occurred to him in the past few days. His mind sought out the whereabouts of his brother, Henri. Was he alive? Was he captured? He prayed to God for answers, but none came to him. Surely among this 'sea of men' God would hear his plea and answer it. On this prayer, he finally drifted off to sleep.

It was very late at night when Jean Paul heard a clamor on deck. It was more than one man and they were stumbling in the passageway just past his cabin. It must be the Captain, he thought, but was too tired to rouse himself to settle the question. Morning would come soon enough and he would find out then.

When morning came, it was the bellowing of the Captain that woke him, "Jean Paul. To my cabin. Now!"

Grabbing his sabots, Jean Paul raced down the passageway to the Captain's cabin.

"There's been a change in plans," began the Captain, "The Bishop has brought bad news from Paris. We cannot go to the Azores. All the nations have declared it persona non grata to pirates and privateers. We are to proceed to the Canaries. Spain will still give us sanctuary. Besides, the East Indies hold much bigger prizes than the islands of the West Indies."

Jean Paul stood with his mouth open, stunned, and then finally muttered,

"But Captain, it is near the end of November and everyone knows the British do not hunt pirates or corsairs in the winter. All their ships are in dry-docks being refitted for the spring. That is why all the freebooters head for the warm waters of the West Indies. The Azores are the quickest way to the American South Seas."

"I know, I know," replied the Captain, "But it's getting too crowded down there. There's no place to get away from the buccaneers and the British. Hell, even the Americans are into every cove, cay, and harbor."

"Besides...," the Captain stopped in mid-thought. He did not want to continue what he had begun, so Jean Paul waited for his conclusion. One could almost see the Captain switch to a new idea on the spot.

"The hunting is much greater elsewhere."

His voice trailed off, "To the Canaries..."

Knowing that the conversation was over, Jean Paul turned to leave the room.

"To the Canaries, then," remarked the Captain, noticing Jean Paul leaving the room.

"I'll let you know where we will go from there. Oh, and one more thing. We have a guest on board, but he will show his face to no one. Tell the cook, he will take meals in his private cabin. The crew does not need to know anything about this, so tell no one. That is all."

Jean Paul was flummoxed. He had just finished plotting a detailed nautical calculation to the Azores and now he must redo them, all without an explanation, except that East India was a richer prize. What Jean Paul did not know was that the nations of the world were slowly facing up to the fact that piracy was an offense against all nations and without a war to justify it, pirating was an unacceptable business for all trading nations. The Captain was going into hiding somewhere, but where was the question. Maybe the secret passenger in the room next to the Captain's knew the answer.

Flushed with anger, Jean Paul measured his pace back to his cabin door. He told no one of the Captain's decision; he would take the ship straight out of St. Malo's harbor, past the British sporadic picket line, into the Atlantic Ocean, where he would formulate a new course.

There had better be gold in abundance for they would be sailing over 1800 miles, around the dangerous Horn of Africa, and passing into the lawless lands of Madagascar. It would cost Jean Paul two, maybe three years of his life.

∽

Canary Island are just west of Africa in the Atlantic Ocean.

CHAPTER 9

When the sun rose the next morning there was no need for Coquelin to fire the morning gun for the tide rushing to the sea pulled all the boats in the harbor toward that goal. Anchor hawsers were straining for relief.

Even the sea birds were searching for food in the freshening breeze. The crew was alive with activity. Pirate sails were doused and the fresh canvas was flapping in the dawn wind. No one aboard, save Jean Paul, knew that a great adventure was about to begin.

From his perch behind the quartermaster, Jean Paul watched intently as the Quartermaster Bateaux, threaded the hundred and ten ton vessel past the buoys, harbor skiffs, and work scows on its way to the open sea.

Safely past the rack and ruin of the harbor, Jean Paul turned from the quartermaster's wheel toward the cabin door.

"My dear God," began Jean Paul slapping his mouth in mid-syllable, color draining from his face, "A ghost. It must be a ghost."

His eyes had met the face of the Captain's guest, a short, squatty, ugly man with a blood-red beard, as he quickly returned to his cabin.

"I know that face," muttered Jean Paul, "I know that body. I know not his name, but I remember the blood. Oh my God. It cannot be!"

"What are you muttering about?" asked Bateaux, the quartermaster.

"Yes, about what, indeed?" added the familiar growl of the Captain.

"My eyes...they must be playing tricks on me. I thought I saw a specter in the spanker sail. Too much wine last night, I suspect." Jean Paul realizing he was talking out loud quickly tried to disguise his astonishment.

His answer seemed to satisfy all present. In that brief moment, Jean Paul knew who it was. He could clearly see the short man standing by the guillotine tying the hands of Brother Benoit ... and the six nuns of 'God's Geese'. God had delivered the 'Butcher of Paris' right into Jean Paul's hands.

The prospect of killing the man was so delicious, it took Jean Paul half an hour to regain his composure and return to his navigational duties; setting a course to the Canaries.

The Butcher of Paris.

Jean Paul would have to wait for a propitious time for vengeance.

The Canary Islands, though under Spanish control, lay south of Spain and Portugal and the mouth of the Mediterranean Sea from the Atlantic Ocean, making it a convenient stopping point for all of the nations bordering the Mediterranean.

First discovered by the Roman Navy in pre-Christian times, it was named Canary, Latin for 'big dog', because of the number of vicious mastiffs that roamed the seven large islands of the archipelago. It lay only one hundred miles west of the coast of Africa. Inexplicably it featured two capital cities, competing for sole dominance of the islands. One was Las Palmas of the Grand Canarias, the other Santa Cruz of Tenerife.

Jean Paul plotted a course between the two capitals and decided to make landfall at Las Palmas. Unbeknownst to him, a British squadron under the command of Commodore Horatio Nelson was sailing parallel to him, with a view toward invading Tenerife. The Spanish defense forces would be waiting for Nelson.

The unusual harbor activity in Las Palmas told Jean Paul that something odd was happening. His suspicions greatly increased when he was called to the main deck to help the crew bring a stranger on board to meet the Captain and his guest. He was a surly, unkempt man who did not even lift his cap when he entered the Captain's quarters, in the company of the 'Butcher of Paris'.

"Well, well, gentlemen," greeted the Captain, "You're a bit early for dinner, but come in, come in. Tell me the news."

The Captain waved the man into the room, and gestured for him to sit, "This is Juan de Fuga. He lives here in Las Palmas and brings us the latest news."

Port in the Canary Islands.

"The harbor is all ablaze with the news. Surely your ship must have seen his squadron on its way to Tenerife? If I were you, I would sail immediately down the back passage of Africa and escape his frigates," returned the stranger, Juan de Fuga, ignoring the Captain's invitation to sit.

"Escape whose frigates?" questioned Captain Moulin-Bleu.

"Why Commodore Nelson's, of course," replied Juan de Fuga, "Did you not know that he left Corsica a week ago? The Admiral knows of the Spanish treasure harbored at Tenerife bursting with South American gold. He means to raid it like a corsair and present it to King William after paying off his debts. He'll bag you too, if you remain here. Commodore Nelson may have lost his right eye in Corsica, but not his brains!"

Jean Paul should have left the room but in the excitement remained to hear all the details, "How big is his force?" he questioned loudly.

Juan de Fuga responded after sizing up Jean Paul, "Four frigates of 74 guns, eight corvettes and a troop ship, I think."

"That's no pirate raid, that's an invasion," replied Jean Paul, "He's going to invade Tenerife, hit the fort and scoop up the gold in the venture.

That's what I would do," concluded Jean Paul.

All eyes slowly turned toward Jean Paul.

The Captain broke the silence, "That's just what we were going to do ourselves. But against four frigates and a lesser host our prize has slipped away."

"I thought Spain and England were on friendly terms?" spoke Jean Paul.

"And so they were," answered the Butcher of Paris, speaking for the first time, "Until a certain French Lieutenant named Napoleon changed the French mind; now England hates Spain as much as France."

"Damn all this international politics," the Captain slammed his fist on the table, "Jean Paul, plot a course for Cape Verde, Africa. We'll leave in the morning. Juan de Fuga, what is the news from Paris?"

Juan de Fuga began, "I don't know if we have time to tell you all the details, but I can tell you that the terror is over. They've beheaded Danton, Robespierre and the whole gang of Revolutionaries. The government is now run by a Directorate and they seem to be leaning towards that same Lieutenant you spoke of, Napoleon Bonaparte. With the terrorists out of power, the killings seem to have moderated a bit but they are still fighting a war on three fronts. Oh and yes, the terrorists gave away the crown jewels to the Prussian Army as a bribe to make them refrain from attacking Paris."

The Butcher interrupted, "You mean they have stopped looking for me?"

De Fuga shook his head, "No, some people will always remember. Your type of evil is not easily forgotten."

Hearing those words, the Butcher slunk deeper into the shadows of the dimly lit cabin.

Peering into the dark shadows, De Fuga continued, "You have many enemies around the world."

Jean Paul eyed the room to size up the disgust toward the Butcher of Paris, but when his eyes met Captain Moulin-Bleu, the Captain bellowed,

"Enough! You may carry on your argument at a later date. We have work to do. Thank you, De Fuga, for all your intelligence. As soon as fresh water is on board we leave for the Gold Coast. By midnight, we'll be off the coast of Africa."

The Butcher of Paris was a curious man. His real name was Zuba Vachem, but his lineage and original homeland was unknown. Although he appeared to be Russian, he claimed to be a French citizen. That he was a Revolutionary was never doubted.

That Jean Paul would kill him, if he had the chance, was certain. Jean Paul would bide his time as his hatred of the man smoldered within him, even as he questioned why this man was allowed on Captain Moulin-Bleu's vessel.

The pirates code was not an easy one to figure out. Befriending outcasts made Jean Paul uncomfortable, and being around the Butcher of Paris made it outright painful.

Captain Moulin-Bleu saw De Fuga to the captain's gig wishing all the while that he was seeing the Butcher of Paris off his vessel. His reasons for befriending the Butcher of Paris were strictly monetary and as soon as they acquired their booty, ties with the monster would be severed.

He instructed Jean Paul to rouse the crew and prepare to set sail for the African coast. Jean Paul smelled the beginnings of bad blood between the Captain and his guest, Zuba Vachem, the Butcher of Paris.

With two hours until sunset the crew set about making the ship's departure as quiet as possible. There was only sixty miles between the smallest and most easterly of the Canary Islands, and the African coast. Jean Paul knew he had better be wide awake to clear the coast and the islands. With a fierce hatred of pirates, Commodore Nelson, even with one eye, could still best the *Diablo Dauphin* in a fight.

What Captain Moulin-Bleu and Jean Paul did not realize was at midnight as the Diablo sailed away from the coast, Commodore Nelson was invading Tenerife, the very place they were just hours before.

This invasion failed but during the battle Nelson sustained a life-threatening wound. His right arm was seriously injured and when he returned to his flagship, his arm required immediate amputation. In a bizarre twist, Nelson's second-in-command, Captain Fremantle, had suffered the same injury, requiring the same amputation.

This uncanny event, where both Commodore and Captain lost their right arms in the same battle, was later discovered to be caused by the enemy miscalculating the sights on their muskets.

Aiming for their enemy's hearts, the enemy shifted their musket sights to the left, causing the bullets to hit the right arms, instead of their hearts.

Commodore and Captain lost their right arms in the same battle.

Commodore Nelson and Captain Fremantle were denied active service for the better part of the year, but Commodore Nelson, now with only one eye and one arm would go on to retain his command as Vice Admiral and defeat the French fleet at the Battle of the Nile in 1798.

Jean Paul stayed awake, preparing for the nautical challenges ahead. The first test after clearing the Canaries was to steer the *Diablo Dauphin* due west to clear the coast of Cape Verde. The green Cape was a misnomer, though. Once a green domain, south of the Atlas Mountains, it was now claimed by the Sahara Desert, dry and hot.

"Thank God," thought Jean Paul, "We have just taken on six tons of fresh water. That should last us slightly over three weeks." He knew that water kept longer than three weeks would turn into a green slime that neither man nor beast would drink. The *Diablo* had three goats on board, but their milk was meager and they, too, would not drink the green slime.

A week passed and then another. The trip was beginning to get tiresome. Jean Paul gazed at the distant shoreline and spotted a desert storm raging over the Sahara dumping tons of windblown sand into the ocean.

The crew's nerves were frayed, and tempers were short. To break up the monotony, Captain Moulin-Bleu allowed an extra ration of rum for all. But this backfired as fights ensued. As the scuffle disbanded, one mariner was found dead with a cracked skull. So, vespers were read and chants were sung as the dead crewman was prepared for burial. A twelve pound cannon ball was tied to his chest and feet, while another cannon ball was wrapped tight to his beltline, making sure that the body would not surface again.

The crew slowly lifted the lifeless body of the seaman and dumped him overboard as he was given the deep six.

A fortnight later, as the *Diablo Dauphin* approached the

A burial at sea.

Bight of Benin in western Africa, Coquelin spotted water spouts ahead of the ship. The Captain ordered more sails crowded on and within a half day of sailing they were directly behind the pod of humpback whales. They were huge, gray monsters, forty-five feet long and blowing their lungs clear of the collected briny water.

"As far as oil goes," began Bateaux, the Quartermaster pointing to the pod, "the whale on your right is the best source. It's called the 'Right Whale'. You can see she's about fifty feet long and full of oil, an easy whale to take."

"You know they float when ya kill 'em… yeh, an easy whale to take. We love 'em."

"How do you know so much about whales?" asked Jean Paul, shouting over the wind as the ship raced toward the pod of whales.

"Was a whaler, once…'fore I came a corsair," replied Bateaux.

"If you want to see a whale worthy of the name, catch a blue whale," interrupted the Captain, "She's almost as long as this here *Diablo*! Close to a hundred feet long and blows near half an hour…takes two vessels to land her. I know a captain who retired from one blue whale alone."

The crew broke out in laughter, hardly believing the tale.

"First man never has a chance!" grumbled Bateaux returning to his duties.

From the time the *Diablo* sailed south of the Tropic of Cancer, the imaginary line of latitude that parallels the Equator, Jean Paul knew he would not see Spring, Winter, or Fall again until he sailed south of the Tropic of Capricorn, a line girdling the globe 23.5° south of the Equator. Between both of these lines, each 23.5° south and north of the Equator, lay the tropics, where the sun at noon, twice a year, lay directly overhead and the unforgiving heat and light never permitted any season but summer to appear. Jean Paul would be a year older when next he knew a spring.

Jean Paul eagerly set a course for the Niger River delta. Although the mouth of the Congo River was closer to the Equator and the heart of Africa, the Gold Coast was even closer to the treasure lodes.

Jean Paul was happy to be exploring again. Besides, shoes, pants, and bandanas were all the clothes they needed in those latitudes and that felt liberating to him. He admired all types of travelers, especially the French and Portuguese. He felt that they were the best explorers of all.

The English, he thought, were rulers and conquerors, the Dutch were traders, the Spanish were missionaries and gold seekers, and the Prussians were soldiers and farmers.

But the French were the best explorers, even better than King Henry's Portuguese because the French were willing to intermarry among the natives they discovered, and in doing so could better trade with those lands.

However, not all European nations approved of this practice. But, Jean Paul could plainly see by looking at the townships on his maps, that in spite of these prejudices, it was evident that the west coast of Africa was covered with the names and languages of every nation in Europe and even many from the Far East.

∽

The Captain grabbed the small spyglass telescope,
and peered into it...

CHAPTER 10

The first warning that action was afoot came from Coquelin. He was stationed at the top of the main mast. The warning was a measured rapping of his cutlass against the wood of the main mast together with a long, low whistle; a technique he developed for alerting the crew to action during a night raid. Even in close quarters with enemy vessels, it alerted the crew without warning the enemy. The entire crew stopped whatever they were doing and looked up at the maintop where Coquelin had lodged himself. Their eyes followed the direction of his outstretched arm. Coquelin had spotted two boats at a distance bearing west northwest. One was a frigate of 74 guns and behind it, portside, was a Dutch cargo ship called a fluyt. Both ships were flying the Dutch colors and looked to be bound for America.

Captain Moulin-Bleu had gotten wind of the sightings and burst out of his cabin grinning from ear to ear, "Give me a glass, Bateaux. I think we've found our quarry."

The Captain grabbed the spyglass telescope and peered into it, "The frigate's a guard and the fluyt carries the gold."

The crew flew to their tasks but wisely did not run out their cannons. They knew the Captain had a plan and did not wish to spoil it by anticipating his solution.

"Back off the mizzen canvas and show them the Jolly Roger," commanded the Captain.

"So soon?" questioned Bateaux.

"I want them to know who we are. Fear is one of our weapons! We can see what they are made of!" returned the Captain.

"Jolly Roger" pirate flag

Then turning toward Jean Paul he commanded, "Steer a course directly behind the frigate, Jean Paul, but be ready to whip staff to starboard on my command. Arm yourselves, gentlemen, this is going to be a man-to-man fight. Jean Paul, grab a sharp boarding staff and be prepared to defend Bateaux, our quartermaster, with your life. Load all cannons and reef all mainsails two points. We're going to shoot under them."

The commands tumbled out of Captain Moulin-Bleu's mouth like guppies out of the mouth of a catfish. To say that he was on fire with excitement was putting it mildly. His whole personality exploded with enthusiasm. For a man in his fifties, this change in aspect was unbelievable as well as exciting to the crew. They had only known him as a static, reflective man, never shaken by events or the excitable nature of his younger crew. But now one could see the wildness of his gray streaked black hair tousling like a battle flag in the wind. His deep set black eyes pierced all who beheld him like two flaming orbs in the night. Action was upon him and battle was its name.

His understanding of the tactics needed for the coming fray were born and polished by eighteen years in the British navy, six of which were served under Captain Hardy, Commodore Nelson's Second-in-Command.

Having been passed over twice for promotion, for which reason he was never informed, Captain Moulin-Bleu resigned his commission in the British Navy and chose the route to riches as a Captain on a corsair vessel fighting for France with 'letters of Marque'. Discouraged again, the Captain's descent into piracy came about a short while later.

The Captain was a portly man and could defend himself in battle with a French rapier, the weapon of an officer and gentleman, although he admitted in the heat of a shipboard melee, the shorter, flatter blade of a cutlass was easier to handle. He also admired Jean Paul's Scottish dirk, from a distance, but knew that Jean Paul would need it to fend off attackers of the helmsman, quartermaster Bateaux, while he maneuvered the large ship's wheel.

The dirk attached to Jean Paul's sash was now a part of him, even though he bought it just ten months earlier in Paris. For Jean Paul, the blade was a constant reminder of the gruesome guillotine execution of his dear friend, Brother Aloysius Benoit.

It was critical that there was no interference with Bateaux while he whiplashed the ship's rudder starboard and then smartly turned it back to larboard.

He meant to crush the prized Dutch fluyt cargo ship between the *Diablo* and the Dutch frigate.

With the bottoms of his main sails mostly furled, the ammunition rounds from the fluyt's four cannons would pass under the *Diablo's* furled sails, and above its gun deck.

Captain Moulin-Bleu's men would then be able to board the fluyt, lay waste to its crewmen and continue on to board

the frigate now lying portside from the fluyt ship.

It was a daring plan, but a simple one. His blood thirsty crew would make short work of the Dutchmen. Those seamen were, after all, solid traders not 'wolves of the sea' like his men.

There were two young Dutchmen who leaped over the *Diablo's* rail and charged for Bateaux, hoping to dislodge his grip on the wheel forcing the *Diablo* to disengage its course. But Jean Paul's long, iron-tipped staff parried their attempts cracking the sword from one assailant and slashing the forearm of the other. Wounded, they quickly retreated.

Meanwhile, Captain Moulin-Bleu and his crew were swinging on the boarding ropes, banging against the sides of the Dutch frigate.

118   *WILD IS THE WIND - RICHARD LOUIS FEDERER*

Jean Paul slashed the forearm of the assailant.

The Dutch captain had seen Moulin-Bleu's plan unfold and began to cut loose from the fluyt and turn to port. Two dozen of Moulin-Bleu's men rode their lines to the flank of the frigate and furiously climbed on board.

Once on deck they slew the helmsman, navigator and captain. Within another ten minutes the leaderless crew hoisted a white flag and surrendered.

The Butcher of Paris rushed down the hold of the fluyt once he saw the white flag of surrender. He was eager to inspect his prize. In seconds, he reappeared on deck shouting, "We're rich...we're rich! I counted two hundred and eighty slaves...unbelievable."

Captain Moulin-Bleu clambered back on board the Dutch fluyt. He knew there were slaves on board. That's what the frigate was protecting.

They could not fire their cannons for fear of hitting the fluyt and killing their precious cargo.

The Butcher of Paris shouted, "We're rich…we're rich!
I counted two hundred and eighty slaves!"

He also knew that when his crew saw their prize, they would be disappointed. Moulin-Bleu and his crew hated slavery.

It stood for a way of life that almost all pirates detested. It was at bottom the reason why pirates had become pirates; to escape from the slavery of society.

The crew, to a man, knew that they would have to set the prisoner slaves free. So, when the Butcher of Paris discovered their sentiments, he went berserk.

A fortune was slipping away from him and he could not stop it. In fact, he preferred to duel to the death any and every man who disagreed with him.

But Captain Moulin-Bleu knew the crew well and knew what had to be done. He would take his fleet back to Africa. Jean Paul would be the one to lead the way with the *Diablo Dauphin*. The Butcher of Paris with his cargo of slaves on the Dutch fluyt would be towed behind the *Diablo*. If the Butcher tried to break away, Jean Paul would be charged with sinking the ship, slave prize and all. Captain Moulin-Bleu would followed behind with the frigate.

Although the Butcher of Paris could captain the *Slaver* Dutch fluyt well enough, he did not enjoy the trust from Captain Moulin-Bleu to sail alone. These slaves must be freed and returned home.

The Captain used Zuba Vachem for his knowledge and experience, but never trusted the man. The Butcher of Paris, obeyed the rules of pirate life only if they led him to money.

Although there was no gold on board the *Slaver* fluyt, there were four tons of cowery shells, the tribal coin of Africa, and that was worth just as much or more than the slaves.

Cowery shells were first discovered off the coast of India and China. They were made into six inch lengths and were of stunning colors; shiny shades of pearl, pink, red, blue, green and white. As jewelry, the shells were strung together on threads of gut-like strings to form necklaces, earrings, and other dress ornaments. In commerce, these shells were the legal tender of Africa, India, China, and the Muslim Coastline. The British and Dutch traded gold for them and then paid the Muslim slavers in cowery shells for human slaves.

A slave purchased for field work brought one-hundred fifty-thousand cowery shells, a household or talented slave would fetch much more. A Tribal Chieftain would tax his male subjects, one-thousand cowery shells per year. His wife, children and bullocks were taxed the same. Cowery shells were used as sovereign coins in Africa until the 1920's.

Captain Moulin-Bleu suspected that the slaves were being transported to the Americas; Venezuela, Brazil, or Peru as plantation workers or to the Carolinas, Georgia, and Mississippi to work the plantations there.

The mere thought of using these men as slaves was abhorrent to the Captain and his crew. Their whole life was dedicated to the adage 'live free and enjoy life even if it meant an early death.' Men were not put on this earth to live their lives in chains. Pirates believed this even though their chosen occupation would eventually lead them to prisoner chains or the hangman's dock. Few pirates became slavers and those that did were never trusted by their colleagues in crime.

The sharp eye of the Butcher of Paris saw an ivory talisman hanging around the neck of one of the black women and immediately recognized the magnificent carved ivory head of a Benin Chief. These Blacks were either from the Benin, Ibo, or Yoruba tribes in Africa. Their artistry would command a much greater price in North America or Europe. He knew his cargo would be worth double the normal price.

Because of the near nudity of the bare-breasted women and the rapaciousness of his crew, Captain Moulin-Bleu ordered the removal of the black men's irons so they may better be able to defend their women. He also wanted Jean Paul to keep a close eye on the Butcher. Given the chance, he would break from the flotilla and head for the Americas.

"Set a course for the Volta River mouth," announced Captain Moulin-Bleu, "That's where the Gold Coast begins, though I suspect most of the gold is gone from the river by now." The Captain eyed his crew.

"We'll set this cargo down between the Volta and the Northern most mouth of the Niger River delta. From there, they can make their way back to Timbuktu or wherever they came from."

At that, the vessel flotilla turned around and headed back east to the coast of Africa. The Captain let Jean Paul's *Diablo Dauphin* take the van or forward position. He had to find the delta. The Butcher's fluyt with the slave cargo came second and the Captain's frigate brought up the rear.

After several hours of travel and nearly two hundred yards from the beach Jean Paul's voice rang out, "Douse all sails. Stern anchor. Launch."

The stern anchor's fluke bit into the sand and held the vessel fast. The *Slaver* fluyt followed suit and the Captain's frigate anchored fifty yards astern.

Row boats were broken out and the natives rode ashore with much glee and shouting. They were back home. Jean Paul, now on shore, shook the hand of their chieftain and pointed the way inland. To make their journey easier he had let the women take as many cowery shells as they could carry.

"So you give them their freedom and our money?" questioned the disgruntled Butcher.

"We're after gold, not Blacks or seashells," replied Jean Paul.

"We'll talk to the Muslims who sold them, and who knows, maybe they can catch them again," interrupted Captain Moulin, warding off a most certain argument.

"I doubt it," continued Jean Paul while waving at the newly freed slaves now scattering into the jungle.

"The caliph, Saleen Ibn Chad, will be the one to talk

to," finished Captain Moulin-Bleu.

"Someone will pay for this," muttered the Butcher under his breath as he walked briskly back to his quarters.

It was a prophesy that went unnoticed by both Jean Paul and Captain Moulin-Bleu.

᪗

Muslims sold slaves to the Europeans traders.

CHAPTER 11

Among the traders of the eighteenth century it had been an indisputable fact for centuries that the Muslim Arabs were bested only by the Chinese in the shrewd art of bargaining. Saleen Ibn Chad was a master at his game; shells for slaves, gold for shells, and copper for either gold or shells.

Jean Paul was rolling all these thoughts in his mind as he made his way across the Cote d'Ivoire when he caught sight of a French pirogue heading for the Gold Coast and headquarters of the slave trade.

Further south from the Gold Coast was the slave coast where most of the slaves were held in a square compound called a barracoon before being transferred to waiting vessels. Slaves were usually fixed together in two's by irons and were bound by neck yoke sticks in chains of four or more. Raids on villages were organized by the Muslims Factors who sold them to the Europeans or Americans. Everyone who could, did join in the slave trade including honorable governmental officials.

It was considered a legitimate business until the 1850's. During that time, millions of slaves were sold around the world.

When Jean Paul reached the hut tent of Saleen Ibn Chad he had his plan worked out.

"I have six tons of cowery shells aboard my ship and I'd like to trade them for copper sheets. The hull of my ship is being eaten alive by teredo worms and I want to careen my ship and cover her hull with copper sheeting. I understand shipworms do not like copper plating. Can we deal?"

Ibn Chad drew a few puffs from his hookah and blew the smoke at Jean Paul.

"That all depends," began Ibn Chad, "covering a hull with copper is lot of weight. Where is your ship? How are you going to careen her? Who is to transport the copper?"

Ibn chuckled as he took another drag from his pipe, "Do you have two or three months to lay her up on the beach?"

Jean Paul knew Saleen Ibn Chad, the Muslim Factor, was already ahead of him and he tried his best to keep up, "I have twenty-five men to haul her. Can you get me more? Maybe some horses to help careen? I'd just be renting them, not buying."

Ibn, the wise Muslim Factor paused for a moment and then leaned in closer to Jean Paul as he continued, "South of the Slave Coast there is an area that could work. The sea runs cold straight up from the pole, but the surf is fast and runs up a slow sandy beach for miles. Lots of bones and carcasses from skinned whales, sea lions and such. It is called the Skeleton Coast. There is a river that runs under the sand to the sea. When the hot sun meets the cold current from the great Southern land, the fog is thick as timber and lasts till noon but eventually the sun burns it off."

Then eyeing Jean Paul over, the Factor finished, "Yes, I think it could work. That would be a safe haven for your ship. Let's see your shells."

Jean Paul knew the shells would be in the very Dutch fluyt that Ibn Chad had loaded before with slaves, but he had to

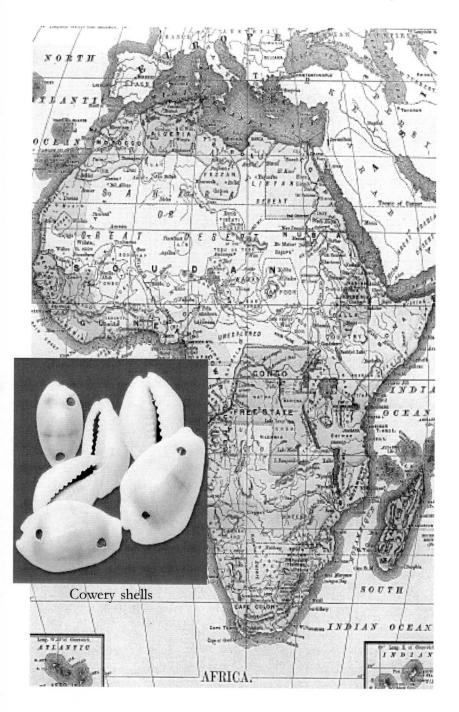

Cowery shells

take the chance and bring the Muslim Factor to his ship.

Jean Paul was grateful that Ibn Chad volunteered so much information about the Skeleton Coast. He knew he could talk him into renting some slaves to help careen the *Diablo Dauphin*. His crew could unlimber the forty-seven cannons, scrape the hull, coat it with sulphur and tar, and cover the hull with sheets of copper shingles to stop the barnacles from attaching themselves and the teredo shipworms from eating through the hull. He had noticed how much slower the *Diablo* had sailed when in company with the Dutch fluyt. That wasn't right. The *Diablo* should have easily sailed away from them. The aging hull was encrusted with worms, barnacles, and rot, but with her new copper plates, the *Diablo* would fly like the wind and he confidently informed the Captain so.

Dropping a third of their shells off as a down payment to Saleen Ibn Chad, the little fleet set sail down the Skeleton Coast to wait for a low tide that would carry them onto shore. Jean Paul knew he was approaching the Skeleton Coast when Coquelin announced the sighting of white whale bones floating and bobbing nearby.

There were also smaller skeletons bobbing amongst the whale's remains.

Jean Paul noticed something else. Although it was only five o'clock in the afternoon, a cold breeze began to blow from the south bringing with it a fog that was forming a bank on the sandy beach to the east and over the ocean to the south. An eerie chill ran down Jean Paul's back. Although it was still warm, he felt the beginnings of a cold day in December.

As the wind shifted to the east southeast, he could hear the plaintive barking of sea lions searching for their young. Were it not for the comforting nod of disbelief from Coquelin,

Jean Paul would have shouted a warning to his crew to retreat. They, too, were frozen with fear. While the other two vessels of the little fleet threw their stern anchors into the sand, Jean Paul gave the order to crowd on more sails and barrel ahead to the enlarging beach. The ocean's tide retreated to the deep. Within minutes there sounded the grinding noise of the boat's bottom scouring its belly on the sand and the boat came to a bone-rattling stop. The *Diablo* was beached. Men leaped over the side to secure it to rocks, large whale bones and trees that were nearby to keep the sea from reclaiming the vessel with the pull of the surf. The cannons could be dismounted on the morrow but for now, Jean Paul wished to signal the Captain that all went well and that he could come ashore, if he wished.

Since the careening of the *Diablo* would take a month or two to complete, Jean Paul felt it necessary to reconnoiter the coast before the fog completely enveloped them.

He ordered Coquelin to form a small party of skirmishers and prepare to follow him ashore.

When the party landed on the beach the fog bank had lowered itself to three feet above the shore so that the entire landing party had to bend their heads down and peer under the cloud bank to navigate the shoreline. Within minutes, however, they could no longer see each other.

Soon they all were hollering at each other to determine their whereabouts. Jean Paul figured he had taken no more than twenty steps when he heard an earsplitting sound, something like a terrified trumpeter madly howling for help. The sound forced him to stand upright. When he raised his eyes up, he met two penetrating eyes and a grey leather trunk.

There, standing on its two hind legs, was a male rogue elephant shrieking its head off, apparently as frightened at the encounter as Jean Paul was.

At that, Jean Paul stepped back and screamed. He wasn't sure if any sound came out of his mouth or if the screams that he heard were his or those of his fellow seamen, but it seemed that they, too, had run into the same herd of elephants.

At all events, Jean Paul quickly turned and ran toward the ocean followed by the disengaged frantic seamen who bobbed and ran like scared children.

Tomorrow, the group would be better equipped to explore the Skeleton Coast and with any luck, the sun would burn off the fog and they would be able to see what was out there.

Within a fortnight, Ibn Chad had made good on his promise. Fifty Benin slaves and two trained African elephants slowly and noisily crashed through the forest.

They arrived almost at the same time as the cannons and other heavy furnishings were disembarking from the boat. Jean Paul calculated that the whole job of careening and repair would be finished by his eighteenth birthday, just two months away.

With the vessel on the soaking wet beach, the careening process began. Huge ropes were tied to the top of the three masts and with the aid of the local African elephants the ship was pulled over onto its side. After the ship was secured, the crew then moved to the exposed side of the ship and began the laborious job of scraping the barnacles, grass, sand and other nautical impediments from the hull of the boat starting at the keel and working toward the topside.

Saleen Ibn Chad had pressed the local Benin tribal men into service and they quickly learned their jobs. But even with

The ship was pulled over onto its side...The crew began the
laborious job of scraping the barnacles from the hull.

additional men, it was a long, slow process made more difficult
by the early morning fog that seemed to keep its captives
immobilized.

Once a week the work crew would build a bonfire on
the beach where they would roast any game that could be
caught between the edge of the beach and the jungle, a distance
of only a few hundred yards. On the other side of this short
stretch of jungle was a pleasant plain at the far end of which
stood a Baobab Tree, said to be the largest of all the trees in
the world. Its trunk was so large that a man could build a two

African Baobab Tree

WILD IS THE WIND - RICHARD LOUIS FEDERER

room house inside and its branches could shelter an entire tribe of Africans. It was considered a good omen for a leader of a caravan to find such a tree for its branches would shelter the entire group for weeks during the monsoon season. Game abounded in the tree and in the nearby plains surrounding it.

The bible called the Baobab Tree the Tree of Life and to Africans, it truly was.

The work on the boat progressed rapidly during the first few weeks as the men labored on the starboard side, but as time went by, they became weary, and Jean Paul suspected that the men were getting bored. Suddenly, the trained elephants stopped working altogether and began to trumpet loudly.

They had heard a familiar sound and responded to a distant call, almost echo-like on the warm soft afternoon breeze. Help was coming and the gray beasts knew it.

Jean Paul and Coquelin dropped their copper plating mallets and ran to the patch of jungle near them. Peering through the jungle foliage they made out a track of six elephants ridden by their mahouts. Silently, the huge behemoths picked their trail through the tangled mass of fallen timbers, bamboo shoots and elephant grass.

As they came closer, Jean Paul could make out what appeared to be over one hundred African Blacks marching in double file. Behind them, still further away, was a lesser number of bare breasted women all carrying spears.

After the women, came a number of tribal elders. Their heads were encased in huge turbans, and their bellies wrapped in many blankets all to give the impression of being very fat. They formed a huge semi-circle around the king with their bodies facing outward.

Jean Paul and Coquelin were frozen with a mixture of fear and curiosity. For a split second they exchanged glances in stark amazement but then quickly returned in awe to watch this show.

As the tribe moved closer, Jean Paul could see that they were heading directly for the Baobab Tree. They now noticed that some of the women had placed a three stepped platform before the Baobab Tree and on top of it was a throne-like seat carved with lion's feet and elephant tails and lined with animal fur. The dressage was just the beginning.

When Coquelin saw the women placing human skulls atop their spears and driving them into the ground on both sides of the throne, his red-skinned face blanched. He had seen this ritual before, half a world away in the West Indies' jungles of Haiti. The natives called the ritual, voodoo. For the first time Coquelin realized voodoo must have come from Africa and the Benin tribe.

Coquelin pulled his head back into the leaves and branches, where he had watched, unobserved. He stared at Jean Paul and violently shook his head in fear.

"Back to camp," he muttered, "Back to camp."

Jean Paul followed him although not knowing why. Halfway to the camp Jean Paul stopped Coquelin.

"Why do we run?" No one follows."

Coquelin replied with one word that he repeated, "Kinkajou, Kinkajou!"

It must have meant something terrible to Coquelin for he uttered the words in abject horror, a horror beyond the grave.

When the two got back to the campfire circle, the fog had descended and a bone-chilling wind encircled them.

The sun had fallen behind a cloud bank while the crew was preparing the evening meal. By the time the sun had set, the meal was ready to eat. Around the campfire torches, the rum began to flow.

Suddenly from the far end of the strand came the sound of tinkling bells, the rubbing of leather shields against spears, and the shuffling of hundreds of feet on the sand. Carrying blazing torches, a double column of ebony men and cowery-clad woman weaved their way through the driftwood timbers, rocks, and bone fragments on the beach. When the column was nearly half-way to the fire circle, the chanting escalated, all singing the same tune, only broken by an occasionally shout. The shifting of the winds gave a surreal effect to the beat only to return to the drum-like chant when the winds died down.

It could have been the rum or just the compelling rhythm of the dancers that enticed the crew seated around the burning logs to forsake their comfort and overpower their senses to join in the chanting dances. After the ghostlike mass had encircled the fire three times, Coquelin finally succumbed to the native invitation. He arose from his seat and joined in the dancing columns. Soon the compelling rhythm got to Jean Paul and he, too, became a Kinkajou dancer along with most of the pirates.

Even in the frenzied state, Coquelin noticed that the dancers were slowly moving away from the log fire toward the patch of jungle. The low moon revealed a coterie of palm-oiled ebony women standing at the entrance to the chief's court. Except for headdresses of white ibis feathers and numerous necklaces of pure white cowerie shells, the women were completely au naturalle.

Coquelin knew that the fervor of the drums would climax and the horror of the evening would begin with the eating of a human, usually a young girl. Throwing himself at Jean Paul, Coquelin knocked him out of the line of mesmerized dancers and held him fast to the ground.

Meanwhile, as the party of dancers had approached the fire circle, one tall native had broken away from the dancers and marched toward the fire. He stopped at the place where Jean Paul had been sitting and addressed Captain Moulin-Bleu who had rejected the blandishments of the dancers and remained in his place by the fire.

Planting his spear near the Captain's seat, the tall native began to speak. Saleen Ibn Chad, who was seated next to Captain Moulin-Bleu translated the words.

"We come, most exalted Chief, to honor you and your men and to help you repair your boat. We are most grateful for the release of our people from slavery so to honor you and most especially your young Chief, this spear shall be the talisman of our friendship, forever."

With that he thrust a beautifully carved eight foot long mahogany lance bearing a three foot metal blade into the sand next to the Captain.

"Tonight," concluded the native chief, "When the moon is high, we will offer sacrifice."

When he had finished he untied a leather bag from his belt, which was filled with a luminous powder.

He sprinkled it over the flames and quickly rejoined the column of dancers while a great cloud of white smoke engulfed the fire circle. A single savage warrior filled the men's bowls with rum and what appeared to be red wine, urging each of them to drink it. It had a bloody taste to it, but no one said a word.

Planting his spear...the tall native began to speak.

"Look what the chief has brought you," the Captain shouted excitedly to Jean Paul, "A genuine war lance!"

Coquelin shook his head repeatedly shouting, "No, no! He Benin Kinkajou! Voodoo! No trust! They eat you!"

There seemed to be a break in the chanting just as Coquelin was yelling. The crewmen near Coquelin fell silent and then quickly rushed to save their shipmates from the dancers now disappearing into the woods.

Soon the frenzied party broke up. Pirates grabbed their reluctant fellow crewmen who were in an apparent trance and dragged them back to the fire. After the commotion of searching for their comrades had settled, the crew rejoined the fire circle and finished their rum, stunned by the evening's events and numbed by its magic. They soon, one by one, closed their eyes, rolled to the ground and fell into a deep slumber. The balance of the evenings' ceremony was lost on them. The Voodoo god, Mawu, had done his work.

When next they saw the sun two days had past, although the groggy crew thought it was just the next morning. As they stumbled into consciousness, they were surprised to see the *Diablo Dauphin* standing erect in three feet of surf and swarming with two hundred natives resetting the mast and rigging and struggling to remount the cannons at the gun ports. With the help of the elephants the natives had finished the copper plating and re-righted the ship in the shallow water. The vision was thought by the crew to be a voodoo trick that would soon dissolve, just as the morning mist would be dissolved by the sun.

Captain Moulin-Bleu properly guessed that the crew had been drugged by the smoke and the blood wine. The Muslim Factor, Saleen Ibn Chad, had slipped away sometime during the reverie of the night, and although his translation skills were helpful, they no longer seemed to be required as the natives appeared to move in uninterrupted unison working on the ship until it was completed.

The Captain was thankful, none the less, for this monumental stroke of luck that shaved a month's time from their careening chores. He was less pleased, when upon climbing to the deck of the *Diablo*, to see a fresh engraving of an African Snake, a symbol of the voodoo sea god, Agbe, sometimes called Hu, carved in the front of the mainmast.

The Benin had placed this vessel under the protection of their voodoo sea god.

Though a fallen away Christian, Captain Moulin-Bleu did not relish sailing under the protection of a pagan voodoo god. He reasoned that every good fortune had a bad fortune connected with it and although these natives rebuilt the ship, he did not want to take any chances honoring their foreign god. He promptly instructed Jean Paul to cover the Snake god using spare wood battens.

What Jean Paul did not know was that the ceremonial lance he was given by the Benin tribe was engraved with the hallowed words of the voodoo god of war, Gu. Inscribed on the edge of the blades were the voodoo words, 'Du Gu Do', which meant 'I Only Kill Accomplices to Evil'.

To Captain Moulin-Bleu's dismay, Jean Paul kept the lance which he had received from the savages as his own private trophy. He place it next to the helm of the *Diablo*. In its own right, the lance was an exquisite work of art.

Coquelin would take it ashore whenever Jean Paul left the boat. He would carry it as a 'knight in attendance' would when near his master.

It would become a visible reminder of Jean Paul's power and authority to all who might do him harm.

Diablo set to sea at the end of the week. The African Benin natives were good on their word, exchanging manual labor in gratitude for their freedom from inevitable slavery in the Americas.

 ↪

Spices from India.

WILD IS THE WIND - RICHARD LOUIS FEDERER

CHAPTER 12

In Vienna, Monsieur DuPrey, resigned himself to ten-hour days of planning and correspondence. He was the Executive Vice-President of the French East Indian Trading Company, and although a revolution might be going on in his country of France, he still had to run the second largest trading company in the world, next only to the British East Indian company.

DuPrey's immediate problem was to assure his Company agents in Rome, Italy, Alexandria, Egypt, Mecca, Arabia, and Goa, India that the French importing firm was still in business. In fact, he was on the brink of signing a contract with a firm in Calcutta, India to build and supply his firm with the largest freighter ever known; a Dutch designed fluyt of a thousand tons burden. The boat was to be built in Calcutta and delivered to him in Goa, India by the Spring.

The ground-breaking design and craftsmanship was uniquely Indian using wooden nails instead of iron ones. When wooden nails became wet, no force on earth could remove them. This innovation proved most effective, for during the monsoons of India these boats were unsinkable. Throughout the world these ships were known as *Indiaman*.

The *Indiaman* merchant trading ship would be one-hundred-eighty feet long, forty feet wide with a crew of two hundred men, manning twenty-five guns. DuPrey needed to purchase fifty iron cannons made in India, five- hundred bales of silk made in China, but dyed in India, and lastly, sixty tons of Indian spices; everything from cinnamon, nutmeg, cloves, and coffee to vanilla, ginger, turmeric, pepper, tea, curry, and green chilly leaves.

Of the sixty spices known in the world, India grew fifty of them. Spices were as precious as gold and used as significant medicines, preservatives, perfumes, and condiments. No country in the world produced as many spices as India, the land of spices, and the palates of the European wealthy had a penchant for them.

Although Monsieur DuPrey's time was spent mainly on work, he found time to write to his family, still secluded at the Christian Brother's Motherhouse in Melun. In his letters, DuPrey only mentioned that his work was taking longer than he expected and that they should stay in Melun until the Spring. He also hinted at the possibility that they may all travel to India with him when it was time to take possession of the new vessel in Goa.

When Madame DuPrey and her daughters received the long awaited letter, the news of travel to India struck everyone differently.

Angelique Marie was eager to leave France right away. She had been cooped up long enough and her wandering spirit needed to travel.

Madame DuPrey was understandably concerned about traveling in the unstable country of France. She had experienced enough during her time at the Saint Sulpice prison.

But Clare Louise, the oldest child, was not happy with it at all. She had made new friends near Paris and seemed to be leaning toward joining their religious group to travel to the Americas as a nun, intending to teach the native Indians there.

Madame DuPrey wrote her husband that she would think on it, but that the trip out of France to Vienna would be risky. Another letter would follow, she advised. She needed to find out more about Clare's new friends. The balance of the letter was filled with the chatter of Paris. Especially how the panic of the last month had settled down after the beheading of the main Revolutionaries.

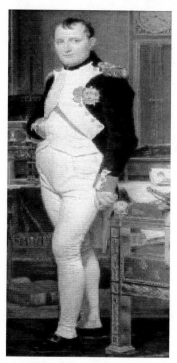

A leader had surfaced among the people of Paris, by the name of Napoleon. He had the control of the directorate but his opposition to the Pope did not sit well with the people. She concluded her letter by announcing that she, indeed, had become the mother of the Motherhouse of the Christian Brothers; sewing, cooking, and cleaning. The Brothers had grown quite used to her help and fellowship, and she fondly referred to them as her boys.

✍

Napoleon became
Emperor in France

The Captain finally settled on the name *Lis de la Mer*, Lilies of the Sea, because she moved so gently through the southern sea.

CHAPTER 13

Nearly two months had passed since Jean Paul arrived on the African coast, and as they sailed the Atlantic coastline of Africa, he remembered that it was his eighteenth birthday. Unbeknownst to him, this event was shared with Commander Horatio Nelson, who celebrated his 18th birthday with the Royal Navy of England, as Captain of his own ship. Jean Paul had not given his birthday more than a cursory thought, for his responsibilities were too weighty.

The fleet of three ships sailed in unison. The *Diablo*, captained by Jean Paul lead the way, followed by the Dutch fluyt *Slaver* manned by Zuba Vachem, the Butcher of Paris, but still being towed as precaution, and the Dutch frigate warship under the control of Captain Moulin-Bleu.

Captain Moulin-Bleu had no affection for his newly acquired Dutch frigate warship and had grown accustomed to renaming his ships to bring good fortune to his travels. After many days of contemplation, the Captain finally settled on the name *Lis de la Mer*, Lilies of the Sea, because she moved so gently through the southern sea.

But all was not right with the little fleet. Captain Moulin-Bleu had come down with a fever that he had caught during their time on the Skeleton coast and he kept to his cabin most of the time. The Butcher of Paris had grown morose with each passing day. He continually missed the daily meetings on the Captain's frigate and was curt with his crew. Jean Paul reported his disintegrating conduct daily to Captain Moulin-Bleu.

When the *Diablo* reached the Cape of Good Hope, Jean Paul could smell rebellion in the air. It was true that the crew had not taken much treasure on this voyage and they voiced their fear that they would return to France with empty purses. Their next opportunity for treasure would have to be Madagascar and to get there they would have to sail through the unpredictable waters off the Cape of Good Hope, which was plagued by contrary and sudden storms.

Jean Paul wondered if they would even get riches there. It was, after all, inhabited by pirates like themselves. When Jean Paul voiced his fears to the Captain, he was shocked by his answer.

The Captain, pale and weak stood up near his cabin bed and roared, "One more score, Jean Paul! Just one more score."

As Jean Paul turned to leave the Captain's quarters, the Captain kept on, "Keep me informed and let me know each day how close we are to St. Mary's harbor. That's our home, Jean Paul. We are safe there. No more kings or queens. No British or French frigates to bother us. We can live out our days in comfort." With that he sank back into his bed.

Jean Paul pondered the Captain's words for a long time. St. Mary's was a pleasant harbor off the northern coast of Madagascar.

He knew that Madagascar was the 'royal home' for pirates. British warships rarely ventured east of the Cape of Good Hope to round the arduous journey from the Atlantic Ocean, and so he knew that government ships of all nations rarely made port there. Madagascar was the 'West Indies' of Africa. With luxurious treasures to live on, it was the new Eden, a prosperous pirate haven. Free from the rules and regulations of civilized life. There was no government to control them, no commands from an unregulated directorate telling them how to live their life, no more taxes to shrink their piles of gold. It was life at sea without the waves and storms. All pirates of Europe wanted to retire there even though it was expensive.

So when the *Diablo* and fleet sailed past the African Dutch colonies at the bottom of Africa, Jean Paul set a course for Madagascar without informing the Butcher of Paris, Captain of the Dutch fluyt, still towed behind the *Diablo*.

It did not take long for the Butcher of Paris to recognize that the sun was rising on the starboard side of his boat and he immediately lodged a complaint with Captain Moulin-Bleu who signaled the Butcher to board the *Lis de la Mer* when they arrived at St. Mary's harbor and to visit him that night.

At the same time, Captain Moulin-Bleu directed Jean Paul to unhitch the Dutch fluyt from the *Diablo* and sail the *Diablo* north around Diégo-Suarez Bay and into the Mozambique Channel to look for evidence of pirate encampments. Jean Paul immediately obeyed and to the astonishment of the Butcher and his small crew, the *Diablo* was sailing away before mid-day.

Before the sun began to set over the African jungle, Zub Vachem's fluyt pulled alongside Captain Moulin-Bleu's Dutch, *Lis de la Mer*.

As was his want, the Captain came to take his glass of Madeira wine at sundown when the sea was calm. He claimed it settled his stomach which had suffered much through his last illness which he contracted on the Skeleton coast. When the Butcher and his crew clambered on board they were fully armed.

"What's this?" demanded Captain Moulin-Bleu, "We have no enemies here!"

"You are mistaken, mon Captain," replied the Butcher, "Seize him, lads, then search out his crew. Your trial will be short and sweet."

Captain Moulin-Bleu struggled to get free from the pirates holding his arms back. He was in no shape to fight them. His illness had all but drained his energy.

"We have been at sea for more than a year with little or no prize or gold to show for it. You have freed captured slaves, taken us to a country we did not vote upon and finally, you have given the *Diablo* to a Junior Officer without a vote from our crews."

The Captain vehemently denied all the charges, especially the last one.

He looked into the familiar faces of his crew, "Surely you remember when Jean Paul first came on board. Surely you remember the unanimous vote to use his navigational skills?"

"No need to plead. We have found you guilty and since no one here objects, you are our prisoner and I will assume the captaincy of this vessel."

Captain Moulin Bleu was aghast and befuddled by this turn of events. The best response he could muster considering the circumstances was, "What will you do with me?"

"Tie him up, lads," shouted the Butcher, "We will leave the *Lis de la Mer* here in the harbor of St. Mary and sail our Dutch fluyt to one of the native villages. There, we will leave the Captain until we have better use of him. Instruct them to only torture Moulin-Bleu, They should not kill him. That task is for me to enjoy."

The small mutinous crew unceremoniously marched Captain Moulin-Bleu to the boarding ladder and threw him into the Dutch Fluyt. They, then, pushed off from the *Lis de la Mer*, leaving the small loyal crewmen behind. The Captain shot a yearning glance at Jean Paul's *Diablo* as it drifted peacefully away into the sunset, completely unaware of the fateful demise of his Captain and his ship.

The remaining crew onboard the *Lis de la Mer* was stunned into silence. There were still on friendly terms with the Captain and did not wish to see him leave, but they kept their mouths shut, for they feared the same fate if they retaliated against the cruel Butcher of Paris and his mutinous crew. This was the way of pirate life. No Captain was ever safe from mutiny.

Even though Zuba Vachem disliked Jean Paul, he still needed a navigator and did not have one on board the Dutch fluyt. The best he could manage with the setting sun upon them, was to follow the wake of the *Diablo* into the fading light.

Cautiously, Jean Paul sailed the ship, which was now rounding the northern headland of Madagascar, to search for some sign of a pirate village. What Jean Paul did not realize was that Madagascar was bigger than France and was the fourth largest island in the world. It laid three hundred miles east of Africa and it would take him months to circumnavigate.

Sailing at a safe visual distance from the stern of the *Diablo*, Zuba Vachem effected an immediate starboard turn toward Africa, a two days journey away. And after trailing the *Diablo* silently in the dark, while Jean Paul and his crew was focused on the shoreline, the Butcher of Paris and his

Dutch fluyt, quietly passed the *Diablo*. It was a mistake having all eyes on one side of the ship, and it cost Captain Moulin-Bleu plenty.

The Dutch fluyt arrived at a Magadoxa, a small native village, north of Madagascar off the coast of Africa, and a place where white men were killed first and questioned later.

∽

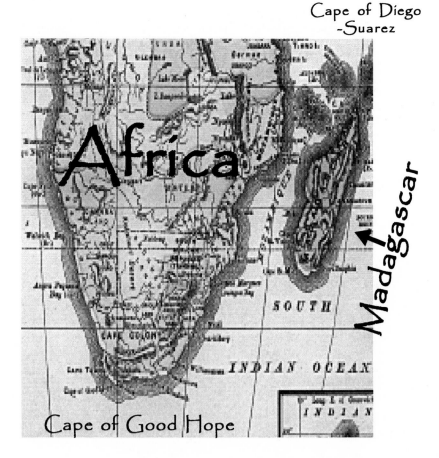

CHAPTER 14

The natives of Madagascar and environs were a mixture of East Indians from Borneo and beyond, native Blacks from Africa, and Chinese from the north. Madagascar saw its first inhabitants around 500 A.D., while pirates from Europe arrived only after the close of the first millennium. Of all the immigrants the pirates were the most influential and the most deadly. They arrived and settled to escape the maritime laws of Portugal, England, France and Spain.

Madagascar became a resupply and replenishment haven for all the 'wolves of the sea' operating in the Far East waters. Muslim and Arabian trading vessels were a good source of treasure, but tales of India's wealth were the most compelling lure even if the stories were not quite accurate. It was believed that the gold of India's empire was inexhaustible and that India contained the only diamond and precious jewel source in the world. Every pirate and government wanted a piece of that action.

From Madagascar, a resourceful pirate, if he was so inclined, could sail north past Mogadishu and the Gulf of Aden, pick up the monsoon trade winds blowing northeast to India, ravish the Indian coast or engage the Indian trade vessels loaded with silk, spices and other treasures and head for Mecca up the Red Sea.

In addition, all Muslims were bound by their faith to make a pilgrimage to Mecca once in their lifetime. When they journeyed they brought all their wealth, including their families, aboard and if pirates happened upon them, their gold and treasure would be a phenomenal pirate prize. The seas lanes to the Red Sea were always full of gold-ladened Muslim ships and hungry pirate parasites.

One successful trip could make a king out of a pirate. The return from India could be just as successful. The monsoon winds reversed their blow every six months so that the very winds that blew them to India would bear them back to the Nile delta six months later.

It was a pirate's dream and Madagascar was the ideal launching point for these activities as well as the perfect permanent residence, unless of course you were a prisoner, like Captain Moulin-Bleu.

Jean Paul sailed around the Cape of Diégo-Suarez again but this time he headed down the Mozambique Channel off the Indian Ocean holding close to the island of Madagascar.

All prudent navigators held their explorations close to the shores of the country they were traveling around, as a result most towns and villages founded on newly inhabited continents were built within sight of the sea.

No captain was naïve enough to ever venture more than a mile or two inland. They had a healthy respect for the sea and its dangers but they had an absolute fear of the dangers that an expedition inland might hold.

Jean Paul's search for pirate towns was no less different from those old nautical nostrums.

If he could not see inhabitants from his quarterdeck he assumed there were none. So it passed that he and his crew missed the villages that the pirates had built inland and when they reached Cape St. Vincent, the distraught Jean Paul decided to turn his vessel north.

Frustrated as he was, Jean Paul knew it wise to stop briefly at Diégo-Suarez harbor to inquire where pirate encampments were. As the *Diablo* approached the shore, about one hundred yards from the beach, Coquelin spotted a most extraordinary sight. A hatless man with long flowing gray hair and beard, wearing a tattered black frock with a crudely fashioned white cross emblazoned on his breast. He was making the sign of the cross in the air over the *Diablo Dauphin* as it dropped anchor. Coquelin called for Jean Paul to witness this curious spectacle. Jean Paul simply smiled when he saw the old man.

"That must be Father Armando de Licata. I'll bet!"

Coquelin turned facing Jean Paul with a questioning look. "He's a priest run out of Rome by the Vatican Curia many years ago. His is a story that I was told as a young boy in my Vendean homeland of France to frighten us into obedience. I forgot what his crime was, but his punishment was severe and he was ordered to minister to the East Indian natives, blessing a bunch of pit vipers two thousand miles from home. I'd like to talk to him, Coquelin. Have my skiff slung over the side and prepare a small crew for me. I will travel ashore and speak with him. Tell our crew that I am searching for a more direct route. That should suffice for now."

As Jean Paul neared the beach he cupped his hands around his mouth as he spoke to shield against the wind, "Hail, Father! And peace to you. I'm a sea rover and come to you for help."

Jean Paul exclaimed "That must be Father Armando de Licata!"

"I know. I know. You are the young navigator on the *Diablo Dauphin*. I have news for you. Come ashore and God bless," replied the old man.

"Really?" questioned Jean Paul, "What could you know of me?"

Both confused and intrigued, Jean Paul jumped out of his small skiff onto the beach, instructing his crew to stay near the boat. The old man looked on, sizing him up.

"All of Madagascar knows you. Even the drums tell of it. What you don't know is the fate of your Captain. I can help you with that," the elderly prelate replied.

"I've been waiting for you here," the old man continued. Jean Paul was astounded. How could this man know of him, of his current tribulations, and indeed his future? A great many questions flooded his mind as he followed a few steps behind the old priest.

The cleric was short of statue, slightly hunched, his skin tanned and leathery, and as the gentle breeze blew, it pressed the tattered black frock against the old man's body, exposing his frail frame. He appeared to be as thin as a rail, but his eyes were intensely blue and alert.

"Come, sit by me. I have a small signal fire burning on the beach."

When the two of them were settled down, the old man began to speak in earnest, every so often peering with his left eye at Jean Paul as he spoke.

"You are correct. I am Father Armando de Licata. The only Christian man in 2000 leagues and yes, I was sent here as punishment for thieving gold from the coffers of St. Paul, outside the walls of Rome. The pontificate considered this a most fitting retribution, stating that if I wanted gold so much, they would send me to a part of the world where men worship gold, and not God."

The father shook his head awhile, gazing downward at the sand for a brief moment recalling the final chilling words of the Curia," If you survive the rigors of Madagascar; the heat, the cannibals, the pirates; and make a few converts out of them within the next twenty-five years, we'll bring you back to civilization, unless, of course, you are resting in the belly of a savage."

"So, here I came, penitent and sorrowful, and here I will wait for my redemption. And, yes, I have learned the ways of pirates, natives, cannibals, the Indian and Chinese customs, their habits, diets, but nary a convert did I make. But I tried! And the good Lord saw fit to bless me in other ways, ways you may not be able to comprehend."

He continued, "I learned about spirits who invade the souls of good and bad men and who push and pull them toward good and evil like puppets on a string. Since I have been here, I have also been gifted with the ability to know things. Things, maybe a man shouldn't know, but were told to me. Things like your Captain being captured by the crew from one of his vessels. He is being taken, even as we speak, across the Mozambique Channel to a tribe in Africa that is very cruel to white men."

Jean Paul sat erect, shocked by what he was hearing.

"Oh, yes and if you had not turned back at Cape St. Vincent, but instead continued toward Africa, you would have caught up with him in two days time. Had you not seen me and stopped, your new pirate Captain would be charging you onward to the bottom of Madagascar in search of the pirate city at the tip of that island, dangling the gold booty to your shipmates as a means of keeping order."

Jean Paul was mesmerized by what the old priest was saying. He did not know the truth of the tale, but it seemed plausible and was the only intelligence he could act on. Would this clairvoyant priest help him to get his Captain back? In a land not fully charted, could he show Jean Paul where to travel, how to get there?

Would he guide him to the hospitable native inhabitants and steer him away from the dangerous ones? Could he even trust this mystic man?

Jean Paul was near panic. He reasoned that he had no choice but to believe the sage priest. And once he convinced himself of that, he began to coax the priest into going with him, trying every incentive he could think of, including interceding with the Pope on his behalf.

He had known Captain Moulin-Bleu for over a year and had regarded him as a friend, someone whom he trusted and respected. The Butcher of Paris could not be allowed to succeed in yet another travesty. Jean Paul's hatred of that man grew even stronger at the thought of him. He must save Captain Moulin-Bleu.

The old Father agreed to take him to where Captain Moulin-Bleu was being held prisoner. To Jean Paul, reaping vengeance on the mutinous crew of the *Slaver* especially its Captain, the Butcher of Paris, became his new obsession.

The Butcher of Paris became captain
of the mutinous crew of the *Slaver.*

CHAPTER 15

Early the next morning the *Diablo* sailed once more around the tip of Madagascar and down the Mozambique Channel to Cape St. Vincent where they turned west to Magadoxa on the east coast of Africa. They arrived early on the third morning.

The sea was calm and the winds were fair. It was a tranquil, summer morning, but not for long. The *Diablo* sailed quietly toward the outlying shoreline, where many mud huts dotted the beach, and old smoldering fires broke the hazy sky.

Jean Paul was in no mood for lengthy, gentlemanly negotiation. He wanted his Captain back, now! But honoring the request of Father de Licata, he agreed to send Coquelin to parley.

Coquelin sailed toward the shoreline in the small longboat with a white flag flapping in the wind, a universal signal that he wanted to meet in peace.

To insure his protection, Jean Paul ordered another longboat with two squads of musket-men to flank Coquelin's boat aiming directly at the native spearmen.

He ordered the two deck guns removed from the

Diablo and re-installed on that longboat and loaded them with grapeshots.

He had the longboat maneuver between the water passageway and the sand dunes. In doing so, the longboat was hidden by the crest of the sand dunes and would only become visible when the natives reached the top of the dunes. With the deck guns fixed at that short distance, the slaughter would be horrific.

A thundering war cry signaled the charge of the natives. Coquelin's parley efforts had obviously failed. When Coquelin's small party entered the rivulet of water that floated the longboat, a hundred or so natives arrived at the crest of the sand dunes and looked down on the smoking deck guns.

With Coquelin's unarmed longboat exposed, and no sign of parley, the accompanying boats fired their cannons loaded with grapeshots onto the shore. Coquelin quickly maneuvered his longboat out of the way of the conflict and waited.

With all guns loaded Jean Paul ordered a full broadside of the quarter mile distant village. Forty guns belched smoke as they fired 12 pound cannon balls into the unsuspecting village. With this rude wake-up call, the village suddenly came alive with natives running to and fro.

The natives' screams could be heard in the streets of the village before they fell dead. The squads of musket-men posted on both sides of the native flanks fired upon the confused and bloody survivors of the native charge.

Jean Paul reformed his ranks with loaded guns and marched resolutely into Magadoxa. The town was his.

Immediately, they found the building that served as a jail and discovered Captain Moulin-Bleu inside. Except for a forced smile on his lips, he was the picture of pain. His festering left leg had been split almost in two by a spear thrust and was now angrily pulsing with purple putridness. Jean Paul immediately realized that his leg had to come off.

The village was in shock. The native guards ran for their spears, lances, bows and arrows, and the few flint locks they possessed. They were not prepared and looked dolefully unorganized as they ran toward the water.

But Jean Paul was not finished. He ordered every third gun to stand down and reload with grapeshot and to await his order to fire. Because he was passing so near to the coastline, he waited until the natives prepared themselves and came closer to shore before his readied guns

"A native spear?" questioned Jean Paul looking over the Captain's wounds. The cut was deep, to the bone, and it protruded out on the other side of his leg. It was long, too, from his thigh to his shin. The spear must have pierced his leg and ripped the skin downward.

"Yes," winced the Captain as he rolled onto the makeshift operating table, "but it was thrown by a pirate Captain."

"The Butcher did this?" questioned Jean Paul unbelievably.

Captain Moulin-Bleu nodded affirmatively, "Just before he ran to his boat."

In Jean Paul's mind, Zuba Vachem had just signed his death warrant.

"I am sad to say these wounds will end my trip to India," moaned the Captain faking a smile.

He closed his eyes for a moment. He had all but lost his strength.

"Leave my precious *Lis de la Mer* with me," cried the delirious Captain, "It will be your reserve if you decide to return to Madagascar."

Jean Paul nodded in agreement, and then turned to one of the seamen in the room, "Quickly, make a travois," he commanded, "Then, hurry the Captain back to the *Diablo* and tell the carpenter to ready his tar bucket."

Very few ships in the 18th century carried surgeons, but they did bring carpenters who doubled as surgeons. After all, both professions knew how to handle a saw. The chance of survival was based on how quickly the carpenter cut through the leg.

If the saw was dull, it would take longer and the Captain would bleed more. It was imperative that the blade was sharp and the tourniquet was tight. Jean Paul knew he had to act fast.

They would use the Captain's shirts as dressing, ripping them in long strips. The remaining stump of a limb would be dipped into hot liquid tar to dull the pain, stop the bleeding, and any further infection.

It was usually months before the stump was capable of supporting the body's weight and the painful fitting of a wooden leg.

When they reached the *Diablo* they drugged the Captain with morphine-laced rum and wine before proceeding with their gruesome, bloody work.

The Captain's painful moans began to subside as the rum mixture began to take effect.

He then started to sing:

> Chantey man, chantey man
> Chantey me a work song
> With cannon flash
> And cutlass slash

My work grows short
My arms grow strong
Pull for home, lads
Pull for home

Chantey man, chantey man
Chantey me a love song
Of ladies fair
And ladies sweet
Who dance the round
With nimble feet
Then flash their eyes
And pout their breasts
Inviting you to share their nest
Pull for home, lads
Pull for home...

The singing of a sea chantey is probably as old as the sea itself. The songs were memorized and passed on by cabin boys, junior officers, and injured sailors, who because of their wounds could no longer work the ropes, yards, sails and naval gear aboard the ship. Nevertheless, the crew often felt sorry for these injured men and prevailed upon the captain to keep them onboard as musical accompaniments to their daily chores.

The chantey songs, though often bawdy, provided a meter and relief from the often tedious and boring repetitive work the sailors were called upon to do. The songs gave meaning and ease to the difficult and often dangerous work that had to be performed.

In his delirium, the Captain reverted back to a chantey song from his youth. Before the last line was spoken, the

Captain lay unconscious and the carpenter then began his bloody work.

When the operation was over, Father Armando de Licata drew Jean Paul aside, "I think we just saved your Captain's life, but at a high price. I want you to know that your actions today wiped out twenty-five years of missionary work. A white man will not be able to land near that village for a generation. Besides, I don't think they would ever have ever eaten him, he's not black enough. Most cannibals believe a white man has to ripen awhile in the jungle before he is edible."

Jean Paul was never surprised by what came out of the mouth of this sage priest. He had too many years on him filled with many more years of experience and knowledge. But Jean Paul was convinced about his decision to attack the village.

"You are probably right, Father, but I have heard too many stories about delaying rescue attempts only to find your victims either dead or carried away when you finally get to them. I may be rash, Father, but my Captain is alive!"

Turning away from Jean Paul Father Armando de Licata muttered, "I wish I had known you in Rome."

"Father, would you rather travel with me down the coast to look for pirate villages or stay and nurse Captain Moulin-Bleu?" asked Jean Paul.

Father de Licata's answer was a surprise to Jean Paul. With a remorseful sign, he replied, "Oh, the Feast of the Undead will be coming this next week. I'd better stay here with the Captain to keep him company."

He then continued, "You go on to search for the pirates villages. If you hear gun fire you will certainly know you are near to them. Besides, I am sure the Captain will need someone to clean his dressing for a few weeks. That's the hardest part."

With that, they nodded in agreement and then parted.

As Jean Paul returned to his boat, he kept mulling over the phrase "Feast of the undead? Feast of the undead?"

Was that really what the priest had said? What was that? He wished he had asked the good Father.

In less than a fortnight, Jean Paul would find out.

ᥲ

Jean Paul put ashore on the east coast of Madagascar
and found pirates killing natives.

CHAPTER 16

The trip down the east coast of Madagascar was purposely slow for the entire crew of the *Diablo* who were searching the shoreline for signs of pirate activity. A half day's sailing brought them to a clearing in the jungle brush where they all witnessed a shocking sight.

Pirates were tying black natives to trees and then fired at them from fifteen paces. Most of the natives died instantly. Those that didn't were summarily shot in the head, a coup de grace.

Jean Paul ordered two of his cannons to fire over their heads. The close cannon riposte startled the killers who immediately halted their executions.

When Jean Paul put ashore he found the pirates were killing the natives for sport and minor crimes of disobedience, and laziness. He dared not intervene because the blacks were either prisoners or slaves of the pirates.

Upon further inquiry the crew discovered that the blacks were digging up the graves of their relatives, cleaning off the corpses, redressing them in silk shrouds and then reburying them. The practice was called the Feast of the undead, and it was practiced by the natives for untold generations. To the natives this was their way of showing love and respect for their deceased family members.

The practice was horrid to even these uncivilized pirates and they attempted to discourage the natives from carrying it out by murdering those who attempted it.

The actions of those pirates were barbaric and reprehensible. Things had gotten out of control. Men would have never even dreamed of behaving this way in Paris. This was freedom from society run amok. Jean Paul could not see either himself or Captain Moulin-Bleu living with such people. If this were the vaunted freedom of piracy, he would have none of it. When Jean Paul's crew reached the pirate village, things only got worse.

The guts of men and animals littered the mud trails that passed for streets. Women huddled in fearful groups coming forth only when the pirates screamed for food. No one washed. Filth was everywhere. The executioner's dock in Marseille was a glorious end compared to retirement in this hell hole.

Although Jean Paul's tour of the village lasted just a few days, he knew that he had to get his disheartened crew away from this place quickly; away from Madagascar and back to the rolling seas as soon as possible. The cries of anguish from the small village filtered through the evening air, but the crew of the *Diablo* had already hastily set sail, never looking back.

"And the Butcher? Did you find him?" questioned Captain Moulin-Bleu when Jean Paul returned to St. Mary's harbor.

"No," Jean Paul replied, "nor did I search for him."

Jean Paul leaned in closer to the Captain, as he lay on his cot, "This is not your land, Captain. You cannot retire here. It is better for you to fight the Spaniards everyday of the year, than to commit your soul to the horrors of this place for the rest of your life. I, for one, would leave your command if you chose to stay."

With those words the Captain sat up, shifting his bad leg into position.

Jean Paul kept on, "We will stay with you until you heal. The crew needs a rest as well. After a few month's time of convalescence, you can get your sea leg fitted. Then we will provision up the *Diablo* and the *Lis de la Mer* and head for India. Surely, life cannot be worse there."

"Sure, sure," replied Captain Moulin-Bleu with a fading voice. His energy was not up to the youthful Jean Paul.

Then looking at Father de Licata, Jean Paul continued, "What say you, Padre? Are you game for some adventure?"

Father de Licata looked at the young man before him and shook his head with a vigorous, "No!"

"My life, or what remains of it, is here, Jean Paul. Working with these natives all these years....I know it sounds strange, but I've come to love them. Their souls are more precious to me than your gold. I may never win them for God, but I'll never abandon them to the evil that they worship. Maybe someday you, too, will find a treasure greater than gold. Someday you will understand me."

Father de Licata was wise, and his words made sense, but he could not bring himself to abandon his mission and papal punishment in Madagascar.

Jean Paul turned his head sideways toward the priest, "How do you mean that, Father?"

"I have learned," began the priest, "that a man is given two chances for love in his life. One captures him in his early twenties; usually it is a woman, but it can be a vocation, a calling of some sort, or as in your case a desire for riches and the sea. I was greatly tempted by those riches, but I was also shown the love of God."

Jean Paul tried to understand.

"Oh my friend, all men who are resurrected after death will know of this truth, some are privileged with this knowledge beforehand," replied the old man.

He then leaned in closer, "Gold is not your game, Jean Paul. Your chance for love was found in Paris. You have already encountered your fate. Yes, Jean Paul, you must find her again. And you will, soon."

Jean Paul tried to stifle a laugh, but it broke thru, "How...how...could you possibly know that?"

"Oh my friend, the love of God shows itself in strange ways. He has chosen to bless me with the spiritual gift of knowledge of the future. Premonitions if you will. Some call it clairvoyance.. For some people...I read their past and...their future. But only through prayer am I able to discern what is real. For you see, this has been my curse, too."

"So, you were not sent here because of money temptations, were you, Father?" questioned Jean Paul.

Father Armando de Licata waited a time before answering. Perhaps the boy was to be his first conversion, "There was a woman..."

Then the Father began in earnest, "Yes, there was a woman, a Contessa, in fact. Contessa Esperanza del Gato. We met at the little garden behind St. Paul's church. I was in charge of the gardens at the church. I found it most peaceful working with the plants and flowers. The voices in my head were at peace there... But my reputation had traveled far and she had heard of me and my gifts of spiritual guidance.

I was a marriage counselor at the Cathedral on occasion. Our relationship was never one of confessor and penitent, hence no seal of confession was ever a issue. She needed my help and because I was able to 'see' certain things, I was quite useful to her. You see, the Contessa was caught in a web of intrigue between her husband and a Duke. You don't need to know the details, but it is enough to say that her husband was a very powerful man and if he found out about her indiscretions...Well...you can imagine what would happen to her.

I began to counsel the Contessa with vapid scenarios of niceness towards everyone in all occasions, slowly removing herself from contact with the Duke. This proved useless for what the Contessa needed was the sharp edge of truth. Sometimes you must be hard-edged if you really want to help a person, a charitable lesson I learned too late. I chose to tell the Contessa what she wanted to hear instead of the truth.

It is enough to say that she could buy her way out of any difficulty by paying off the Duke. But she could not use her own money to do so. She would donate to the church and I in turn would pay off the Duke. A stupid mistake for me, but she was beautiful and I still believed she was sincerely remorseful for her actions, so I felt compelled to assist her.

You see, I was the Bursar of St. Paul's and had control of the purse strings. We would meet in the garden to work out the details of the loan to

The Contessa

be used to pay off the Duke, so that he would not talk.

What I did not know was that those ivy-covered grey stone walls had ears and that began my downfall. The milieu in which I existed was one of extreme gentility and politeness, but in the end I was used as the escape goat and she moved on, unscathed.

So, here I am lecturing you about the dangers of love. The world knows only of my predilection for gold. They think I stole the purses of the church for my benefit, when in fact I was trying to help a helpless soul. But enough of my past. I hope I told you just enough to satisfy your curiosity."

Jean Paul thanked him for his honesty and they shook hands before parting. A friend, Jean Paul would never forget.

Nodding towards the Captain, Father de Licata said, "Keep his wounds clean and his life, too, Jean Paul. If you can."

Jean Paul thought it, but did not give his thought voice, "Keep me in your prayers, too, Father."

Long after they had set to sea, Father Armando de Licata remained in Jean Paul's thoughts. How did he know that he had already found his love on the road to Paris?

How did he know she was more precious to him than gold? Was the priest really clairvoyant or was he just guessing correctly?

He wondered how much he had revealed about himself to the mystic priest during the time they had spent together.

&

CHAPTER 17

Jean Paul set a course for Mogadishu, a city in Africa near the Red Sea and the Gulf of Aden, in the shadow of Mount Kilimanjaro. This region was called the Horn of Africa because the physical features of the area revealed an outline of a rhinoceros head and horn.

Mogadishu was a thoroughly unsavory collection of mud huts occupied with an even more unsavory collection of cut throats, thieves, and pirates whose main profession, after cutting the throats of lost travelers, unarmed adventurers, well-healed explorers, and occasional incautious clergymen, was killing camels for meat. The offal of dead camels littered the streets of Mogadishu and the stench from this unregulated industry reached a full two miles out to sea.

Though the city had adequate docks, seaborne visitors favored staying well out to sea preferring to send their longboats with passengers and cargo ashore without the ship landing at dock. Jean Paul was not taking any chances with the *Diablo*, so he dropped anchor and waited at the two-mile limit.

It was also important that they stopped off the coast of Mogadishu and not venture closer because the monsoon winds were beginning to pick up. It was soon time for their annual blow toward India. Making landfall during these torrential rainstorms would be impossible to navigate without a knowledgeable guide on board.

During their stay in Madagascar, Bateaux, the quartermaster, had met a man who called himself, Henri. This man, Henri, and his friend, Ralwi Pindar, were familiar with the course to India and had told the crewman so, and both men were now living in Mogadishu.

"Henri? Did you say his name was Henri?" Jean Paul questioned Bateaux.

He attempted to hide his excitement. Could this Henri person be, in fact, his own brother? Henri DeBrosse? In these parts of the world? He knew his brother was resourceful, but after the Anatole explosion, could he possibly still be alive? Could his brother have survived that awful explosion? Henri, Henri DeBrosse..alive!!!! Jean Paul immediately summoned for the services of the man named, Henri.

It was with pleasure, then, that he saw a small boat with two men bobbing toward them from the stench-laden shoreline. When the skiff came within hailing distance, Jean Paul grabbed the nearest ratline and shouted, "Henri...Henri de Brosse? Is that you?"

"None other," came the reply, "Me and my Indian guide, Ralwi Pindar at your service!"

The skiff could not get to the ship fast enough for Jean Paul.

He was so excited, stunned and amazed, but his brother, Henri, had no idea whom he was speaking to.

"Well, I'm the Captain of this ship, the *Diablo*, and my name is Jean Paul de Brosse," returned Jean Paul.

With that, they both broke out in a gale of laughter that did not end until they were escorted into Jean Paul's cabin with a mug of rum in their hands.

Ever the story teller, Henri recounted his capture at St. Malo, after their boat was sunk by the British, his impressment into the British Navy, their attack of the French fleet on the Nile in Egypt, and his eventual desertion from the British fleet after the battle.

He followed that story up with his flight down the Nile river with a crew of French expatriates on a French lateen corsair that sailed to the Indian Ocean, landing finally in the hell-hole called Mogadishu. There he was fortunate enough to meet Ralwi Pindar, an ex-diamond and gold miner from Golkonda, India.

Slapping the back of Pindar, Henri rejoiced, "He'll get us there and back with pockets bursting with treasure!"

Ralwi kept nodding, yes, all through the Henri adventure story. When Henri finally stopped, all eyes moved to Ralwi Pindar, the short, dark-skinned English-educated translator, who simply stated, "I speak very good English."

"So, tell me about your travels, little brother. When we get to the Gulf of Aden we'll turn the conversation over to our Indian friend," smiled Henri as he grasped his younger brother's arm.

"I will," replied Jean Paul, "as soon as we get out of these terribly, smelly waters."

"Go out a mile or so," replied Henri, "and then travel north to the Gulf of Aden. We should pick up the monsoon trade winds there."

Holding a northern course was proving more difficult than Jean Paul imagined. The northeast monsoon winds were starting their eastern blow and a squall line loaded with rain began to pelt on them.

Jean Paul ordered the crew to shorten sail leaving only one sprit sail and the spanker sail to drive the *Diablo* toward the darkening sky. When next they got a chance to talk, the coast of Africa was but a hazy blue line astern.

"I sorry we missed Dubai," blurted Ralwi Pindar, "Dubai is where all the gold of Asia is collected, counted, and shipped to Goa in India, Lahore in Punjab, Pakistan, and sometimes to Calcutta. India imports much gold from Dubai."

"I thought India sent most of their gold to the west," replied Jean Paul.

"Not so," replied Ralwi Pindar, "India hordes the gold it gets from selling spices and silks to the world. It produces diamonds but not much gold. Traders pick up gold in Dubai to purchase spices, silks, and diamonds from India."

"Ralwi Pindar should know, he was once the translator for the Mogul empire to the western world, and he knows quite a bit about the diamond mining business. He is very reliable, brother," returned Henri.

Jean Paul had always trusted Henri and he had no reason to question his judgment now.

∽

CHAPTER 18

Sailing north toward the Gulf of Aden lay a group of islands in the Indian Ocean called the Socotra Islands. Lying 10° north of the equator, this small archipelago of four islands would be the last land that Jean Paul would see until he found the Laccadive Islands and coral reefs off the southwest coast of India. Both island groups lay almost on the same parallel slightly south of Goa, a city and territory larger than London or Lisbon.

Goa was the farthest territory ever reached by any Christian apostle. It was St. Thomas the Doubter who traveled there. When Jesus' mother Mary lay dying in Ephesus, Turkey, word was reputedly sent out to all of the Apostles to return quickly to Ephesus. All the Apostles, except Thomas, arrived at Mary's bedside before she died. Thomas, always the tardy one, arrived late from Goa after her death.

A millennium later, St. Frances Xavier, S.J., was martyred in Goa, India, trying to convert the Muslims. Goa was conquered by the Mongol Empire and was ruled by them for two hundred years. Eventually it was conquered by the British.

Catching the monsoon winds early in the year meant sailing north past the Gulf of Oman and the Persian Gulf.

Turning south towards Bombay, over the Arabian Sea, one would arrive at the port of Goa, which lay below the feet of the western Ghats Mountains.

With the monsoon winds blowing sheets of rain behind the vessel, it was a wild ride indeed. Only twice during the month-long voyage did Jean Paul catch sight of any other ship and that was only a brief glimpse through the driving storms and blinding mists.

Then suddenly, it was there! A ship! A ship so huge it looked like a hulking ghost against the dark sky. Jean Paul started to crowd on more sails, to catch up to it, but the monster had disappeared into the sea clouds. He knew he could catch her once the weather had abated, but for now he had his hands full keeping the *Diablo* afloat and on course.

A storm at sea is a frightful thing. One had to believe in God's love for sailors or the utter capriciousness of fate. The waves had turned back and rolled themselves into gargantuan pillows of death. A stinging spray flew from their crests. Every seventh wave or so was twice the size of a normal wave and this rogue wave threatened to bury the little *Diablo*.

The lips of all the pirates were moving in silent prayer especially those whose duties demanded they be on deck. It felt more secure down below, so everyone tried to hide there. With Captain Moulin-Bleu gone, it was Jean Paul and Bateaux, the quartermaster, who had to remain on deck and bear the brunt of the deadly wave onslaughts.

Suddenly, off the starboard bow they saw the immense hull of the *Indiaman* parallel to them.

Focusing his eyes on the top of its main mast, Jean Paul could make out the welcoming white flag of the King of France, not the tricolor flag of the French Revolution. It was a relief to see the white flag waving along side the royal colors of the French East India Company. She was riding high in the seas which meant that her hull was empty. Although there was port holes, no cannons were visible, which meant the huge vessel was on a shake-down voyage, making her first sea trial trip before delivery to her eventual owners. This was a comfort to Jean Paul, knowing this vessel was of no threat to them.

Just as he lowered his spyglass, Jean Paul noticed something behind the French ship. He looked further to starboard and saw a familiar fluyt tracking the *Indiaman*. It was the Dutch *Slaver* fluyt under the command of Zuba Vachem, the Butcher of Paris. There was no doubt of what he saw. She was not loaded at all. There was no gold or treasure onboard.

Jean Paul had not seen the Butcher since he kidnapped

and nearly killed Captain Moulin-Bleu in Africa, and as far as the Butcher knew, Captain Moulin-Bleu lay dead in an isolated African village with a spear through his body.

The thought of the murderous Butcher caused Jean Paul's blood to boil. Jean Paul was not finished with the brutal assassin, and he intended to pay him back for the injuries to his dear friend.

Jean Paul double-charged a forward cannon and though he knew he was out of range from the *Slaver*, fired the gun hoping the noise would at least scare it away, giving the *Indiaman* time to break away. After two more rounds, the *Slaver* veered away and into the gloomy storm.

The *Indiaman*, now aware of her trailing predator dipped her colors towards the *Diablo* in gratitude. For the balance of the voyage to Goa, Jean Paul lowered the Jolly Roger from his flagstaff and ran up King Louis' white ensign royal in its stead. He placed his vessel on the starboard beam of the *Indiaman* and followed the massive ship through the unruly waters. This new friend at sea would one day prove fortuitous for him.

∽

CHAPTER 19

During the voyage, Henri and Ralwi Pindar had become even closer friends. Ralwi's was intent on showing Henri the diamond mines where he had labored as a boy before he became a seaman. His family lived near Goa in Golkonda where the diamond mines were located. Having spent many years away from his home, Pindar wanted to return.

Henri knew that Goa's ports were used for the transport of diamonds, avoiding the costly and dangerous Silk Road caravan routes and he also knew that India's diamonds were prized for their size and beauty. The mines of Golkonda had produced numerous diamonds including the famous Hope diamond and the rare Daya-i-Nur (Sea of Light) diamond, a blue 186 carat diamond, plundered by Nadir Shar of Persia, during the 'Sack of Delhi' in 1739, sixty years earlier.

Henri, still a young man himself, was drawn to India's tales of adventure and riches. The titillating tales of Sinbad, the Thousand Myths, and riches beyond his wildest dreams, had Henri quite intrigued by Ralwi's offer and when the *Diablo* had docked in Goa, they took off for the nearest tavern intent on returning to the diamond mines of Ralwi's youth. They slip over the *Diablo*'s deck and disappeared into the night. Henri

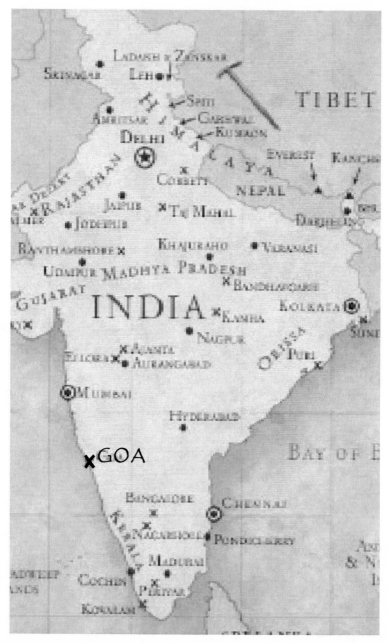

Goa was a Portuguese port city on the southwest coast of India.

was off again, forever a free spirit.

The road to Ralwi Pindar's village ran six miles along the Indian ocean shore and then turned abruptly into the jungle. It was along this coastal road that most of the daily life of India took place. Local fisherman docked and repaired their nets, boats, cleaned and sold part of their night's catch to the early morning shoppers. Babies were bathed along with their mothers at the waterfront, bull and holy cows were watered and scrubbed clean there as well. Freshly dyed Chinese silks were left to blow dry in the sea breeze.

Ralwi and Henri took in all these sights as they proceeded south along the shore. Ralwi was actually searching for a stray donkey or jackass that they could ride to his home in Golkonda. He remembered that there were merchants who would rent them for a few dinars. When a donkey arrived at its destination, its passenger would simply turn the animal lose and it would find its own way back to the seaside stall.

While Ralwi was engaged in striking a rental agreement for two donkeys, Henri became entranced by three smoking pyramids of burning wood. Their strange odor told Henri that this was more than a standard sacrificial fire. Henri then noticed three women suddenly disrobing, in front of each pyre. The women were actually going to throw themselves into the burning flames of the suttee.

Observing the rapt attention of Henri toward the burning sacrifice, Ralwi put his arm on Henri's shoulder and quietly began to explain.

"You are watching a Hindu burial custom called, Suttee. The noble cast of women believe that this honorable act of love and devotion will provide eternal happiness for the couple. It is voluntary on the widow's part, but lately it has become enforced, especially since there is a strict ban on remarriage for Hindu women. The British have forbidden the practice of Suttee but old habits die slowly."

As they mounted their donkeys, Henri could still hear the screams of the women as they fell into the flames embracing their husband's corpses.

Stunned, Henri looked at Ralwi and shook his head. It was a sobering thought that Henri did not want to ponder. He began to realize that he was in a world he could never have imagined.

Not long after that, Henri and Pindar arrived at the mines of Golkonda. At the diamond mines, Henri found digging

A Hindu wife was expected to throw herself into the flames of her husband's funeral pyre.

diamonds to be fairly easy work, unlike searching for gold. Henri would flush the shiny stone specks from the gooey blue clay pipes by scrubbing them until a diamond poked through out of the mud. Further washing would reveal how precious the stone was. After recovering a handful of these stones, Henri would run to the buyer's shed where they were valued and sold. Although quite precious and admired, diamonds were undervalued in India. In fact, they were used as decorative stones in the ceiling and walls of the Taj Mahal, where they remained until the British came and removed them. The Taj Mahal, built for the third wife of the Shah Jahan, was said to be more beautiful inside than out because of these brilliant gems.

Time passed quickly for Henri as he stuffed his pockets with the precious stones and improved his wealth, and although Ralwi Pindar was an excellent host, Henri knew that he could not stay. The lure of the ocean and his home would pull him back, but not until his pockets were full.

৵

The Taj Mahal built by Shah Jahan.

Basilica of Bom Jesus in Goa, India

CHAPTER 20

From at least the time of Columbus, two-hundred years earlier, it had become the custom of all Christian sailors who safely completed a sea voyage, to celebrate their salvation from the sea with a Catholic mass of thanksgiving.

As luck would have it, Jean Paul was just passing by the Basilica do Bon Jesus, or the Basilica of Born Jesus, in Goa India, where the crew and owner of the brand new *Indiaman* were leaving the Cathedral after offering such a mass of thanksgiving.

Jean Paul had heard that the Basilica held the mortal remains of St. Francis Xavier, a Jesuit missionary who died in Goa in 1552 at the age of 46. Since meeting the old priest, Fr. Armando de Licata, in Africa, Jean Paul's curiosity with missionaries had grown.

These men were different from any other he had met, and he found their lives to be intriguing. He sought out the church as a curiosity, but as he came closer to its doors, he slowly became more drawn to it.

Jean Paul was just about to enter the Basilica, when DuPrey and his crew were leaving.

Mr. DuPrey, who was leading the congregation out of

the church, noticed Jean Paul first.

"Ah, Monsieur Jean Paul, " remarked DuPrey, "I come here to pray and give thanks for our safe voyage home. You, my friend, were named specifically in my prayers. Your assistance has twice save me from unpleasant situations. Have you been in the church?"

"Ah, no," replied Jean Paul, "I was just admiring the crowds and the building."

"Well, when you are through, come and join me for a glass of wine. I owe you a great debt. You saved my life in Paris and now in Goa. You have spared my ship, the *Indiaman*, from pirates. I must show you my gratitude."

"Oh, I cannot right now, but I can join you this evening, if that is agreeable," replied Jean Paul.

"Very well then. We will meet for dinner at the Gymkhana Club at sunset. Do you know where it is?"

The Gymkhana Club was an extension of the exclusive East Indian Gentlemen's Club, a private, members-only club established by the elite upper class. Membership to that club was strictly by nomination. In India, however, employees of the East Indian Company were its primary members, allowing Monsieur DuPrey the authority to invite a guest such as Jean Paul.

Jean Paul was vaguely familiar with this kind of club and he nervously responded, "Yes. I will find it."

He knew that this would be an important meeting and so he quickly returned to the *Diablo* to polish up whatever formalwear he had acquired along the way.

He owned a long maroon jacket with a gold sash belt, black pantaloons, a white dickey shirt, and a pair of old leather boots.

His hair had grown long and matted and he had become accustomed to wearing a bandana to cover it up. He would have to wash his hair and cut some off before the meeting.

It was nearly five o'clock in the evening when Jean Paul arrived at the Gymkhana Gentlemen's Club. He walked slowly up the steps and took a deep breath just as the doorman swung the large wooden door open for him. It was even more decadent inside than he had imagined. The foyer was large and its ceiling was vaulted three stories high. In the center hung a large, golden candelabra supported by several long cords that extended down from the very top of the ceiling. The woodwork, balcony, and staircase were all carved from Tai mahogany wood, deeply polished to a rich Oriental patina. Jean Paul could smell the sweet odor of cigar and liquor coming from a room to the left. Its muffled sounds were the only noises in the entire building. He started to walk toward the sound of hushed voices when he spotted Monsieur DuPrey alone in a room.

"Come, come, Jean Paul," Monsieur DuPrey called out.

Jean Paul walked in slowly toward the table where DuPrey sat.

DuPrey motioned the Indian waiter for more wine as he entered, "Please sit down, Jean Paul."

On the table was an ink well, a pen and other writing instruments of burnished gold. Monsieur DuPrey had been writing in a large ledger book.

The table and chairs were of the same rich Tai mahogany wood as the magnificent walls in the drawing room. The windows were fashioned of old English bottle glass sealed in lead and bronze. The clamor of the street traffic was muted by the Indian style curtains made from richly dyed pink Chinese silk. No one else was in the room.

The waiter returned rolling a cart with Indian delicacies, crystal goblets and gold plates. It was a indulgent setting, extravagant enough for a private dinner between a king and his royal minister.

Jean Paul stared in awe of the room, the setting, and the man. Trying to hide his meager nautical accoutrements.

Lifting his glass of Madeira red wine, Monsieur DuPrey began, "As you know I am in the importing business, and we are quite successful. Why one ton of my spices is worth three tons of your gold. Spices from India have seeped into all the wealthy palates of Europe. We supply spices and condiments that the world has come to demand. All of Europe is willing to pay any price just to have a taste of them. I have a warehouse here in Goa, and its contents are worth more than all the gold in France."

Jean Paul sat riveted in his seat, wondering where this conversation was going.

The waiter returned with two large, grilled lamb quarters.

DuPrey ripped the meat off the mutton and began to eat. Jean Paul followed his lead.

"I know you are a pirate, and a damn good one at that. Ha! But you surprised me when you flew the King's colors, knowing that he is dead, and there is revolution in the air. That, my friend, was a bold move that few Captains would do, be they pirate or not.

But I am warning you. You have a problem. You see, pirating is falling out of favor. Every legitimate country has joined an accord to banish and destroy all pirates. Your time is limited in that profession, Jean Paul."

Jean Paul had seen the worst kind of pirates in Africa

and was aware of their cruelties around the globe. He had seen the hangings at the death docks across Europe. Sooner or later the fever of piracy would burn out in favor of trade.

"Remember the ship that you saved a few days ago at sea? That was mine, the *Indiaman*, and it was on its maiden voyage. Before I fill it with a fortune worth of spices, I wanted to make sure that it would sail properly. I did not have an entire crew on board, and was unfortunately not prepared for battle with a pirate ship at sea. Although I consider myself savvy in the business world with those forms of pirates, I am not as familiar with the ways of pirates at sea. So, you see, I am quite grateful for your help and I am quite interested in your knowledge. You could save me a fortune with your knowledge and sordid friendships.

My warehouse holds enough spices to fill the *Indiaman* several times over and one shipment from the *Indiaman* is enough to satisfy Europe for a year. My concern is the safety of the cargo in this part of the world. I need an experienced Captain, who knows the ways of the pirates. To have such a leader, one who has lived on the other side of the law, who could ensure the safe and timely arrival of this precious cargo, I would compensate greatly. I have not forgotten your daring service to my family with the escape from Melun, and the sanctuary you provided at the monastery there.

This is the kind of loyalty and courage I need in my captain. I would need to know that he is honorable and trustworthy, and that he would not run off with my cargo."

Jean Paul was fixed to his seat. His hands on his lap began to sweat. He said not a word, but listened intently. Monsieur DuPrey, on the other hand was still quite relaxed and in control of the conversation.

He took a sip of his wine and then continued, "The route from Goa to Europe is treacherous and long. I would be willing to pay half of the profits from this cargo to a competent captain who could dock the *Indiaman* safely in port. Now, Jean Paul, I ask you, is that a prize worth giving up pirating for?"

Jean Paul nearly choked on his response. A cargo three times the value of gold he could carry, and all without firing a cannon. Now this was a booty his men would go for.

Jean Paul stuttered, "How could I say no to that? When do we load? When would we sail?"

A confident, broad smile filled DuPrey's face, "We're loading now and you will sail in one week. I'll have my agents draw up your papers."

They then shook hands. Dinner had just begun, but Jean Paul was not the least bit hungry anymore. His stomach was full of butterflies and all he could think about was the adventure ahead. In an instant, Jean Paul the pirate, became Jean Paul the spice trader, and a wealthy one at that.

Monsieur DuPrey on the other hand still had an appetite and with the business end of his meeting over, he relaxed a bit.

"Tonight there is a party that I want you to attend, Jean Paul. The newly built Russian battleship, Victor, is in port here. It will guard merchant ships like mine from pirate activities in the Indian Ocean from here to the Gulf of Aden. The distinguished commander Fedor Ushakov is christening it and he is someone you should get to know. Be prepared, Russians throw quite a party! This evening will be unforgettable."

❧

CHAPTER 21

Jean Paul walked toward the harbor to find the Russian battleship, Victor, but he did not have to search for long. The sounds from the party echoed off buildings and nearby ships alike. The Russian frigate was decorated like a Christmas tree. The noise from the band playing in the officer's quarter was mixed with voices and dialects from every nation. Candles were ablaze in every passageway and at each entryway a Russian flag waved joyfully in the wind. Even the narrow repair passageways were illuminated with candles. With the low glow of the cabin lights the effect created a magical maritime ball. It was a magnificent display of Russian décor and royal imperialism. This was the Russia of the czars. Imperial Russia did not dedicate a new battleship every day and the Eastern Empire found it a glorious event.

As he neared the ship Jean Paul could make out the silhouettes of women dressed in their finest and gentlemen from Russian officer to French and Spanish seamen lining the rails and riggings of the ship.

The women and wives, of course, were purely interested in showing off the latest European fashions, flaunting gowns from Paris and Spain, and so from bosom to bodice the new

Thr Russian battleship, *Victor*, was hosting a party.

style trends of Europe were on display. As the women paraded through the corridors to the dance floor to show off the latest promenade from Paris, all the eyes of the on-duty sailors followed them, abandoning their stations.

The Russian officers delighted in flaunting their new ship to the foreign dignitaries and future British Raj alike who flocked aboard to see the latest in Russian military hardware. It was inevitable, therefore, that a party of this repute and magnitude would also draw all types of scoundrels. One of them being the Butcher of Paris, Zuba Vachem.

In the main room, dozens of tables were overflowing with plates full of Russian delicacies, cakes and bottles of wine, and at one of these tables, Jean Paul spotted the Butcher of Paris. Well groomed and elegantly dressed to the nines, Zuba Vachem offered decadent Beluga caviar to a group of French officers, who were mesmerized by this fluent, charming Russian. As he spoke, he sipped on a small glass of vodka, waving his hands in gestures that caused an explosion of laughter from the French officers surrounding him. If Jean Paul had not known Zuba better, he would have thought him to be a high level Russian official, and a charismatic one at that.

No one at the party knew that Zuba was the Captain of the Dutch *Slaver* that attempted to pirate the *Indiaman* just days before. Certainly, if Monsieur DuPrey had known, Zuba would be sipping water through a straw in the belly of an Indian prison instead of drinking vodka from a crystal goblet at the most elegant of parties.

Zuba Vachem, a Russian patriot himself, had acquired a vast number of connections over the years and so he managed to secure, in a short period of time, an appointment as a Russian commiserate in Goa as a supplier. He had weaseled his way back into the legitimate world of trade, as he had done many times before. But for all his showmanship, the Butcher of Paris could never maintain that facade for long. He would eventually return to his murderous ways. And Jean Paul knew it. He would wait. This current performance from the charming Russian would not last long. Zuba was unaware that Jean Paul was at the party and that was just fine with him. He would wait.

Jean Paul backed out of the large room and made his way through a narrow passageway. His mind began to spin as he thought of the many ways to payback the vicious Butcher.

Suddenly. from across the room, a richly paneled door slid open, exposing a stunning example of French womanhood. It was Angelique Marie DuPrey!

She stood regally in the doorway, her soft brown hair piled atop her head. Her dress was made of Chinese silk. The upper half dyed a soft Indian blue, while from her bosom, wear it was tightly gathered in the French Empire style, it fell in a long cascade to the floor in folds of sheerest white.

She had just stepped into the room when a chorus of assembled soldiers and sailors both officers and enlisted, began to shout "Angelique, Angelique DuPrey...sing for us!"

With a sweeping gesture ending in a nod to the pianoforte player, Angelique began to sing in a soft soprano voice, first in English, then in French. When she had ended her song and the crowd begged for more, she continued singing the French song, "Entrez-Nous." She knew the song was flirtatious, and she sang it that way as she slowly circled the room.

As she finished the song, through the thundering applause that followed, she heard the voice of her father, "Angelique, are you coming?" She hastened to join him.

Partygoers were jostling each other in the passageway

Angelique, with a sweeping gesture, began
to sing as she slowly circled the room.

and bumping into Jean Paul, but he ignored them, lost in his
thoughts. Then suddenly no one was there and the hallway
became quiet. He looked up slowly and saw a dainty figure
draw closer. By the dim candle glow he noticed her familiar
face as she approached. Then, slowly, she turned her gaze
toward Jean Paul.

To his surprise, Jean Paul whispered a aloud a longing,
"Angelique!"

She walked closer to him just as stunned and excited as
he was at meeting up again.

Angelique then began to blush, hiding her face in her hands, in a failed attempt to suppress her excitement. They both shifted sideways when they realized the corridor was not wide enough to allow them both to pass.

Angelique Marie began to giggle.

"If we both take a deep breath, I think we can squeeze through."

Jean Paul still in shock nodded yes as he smiled from ear to ear, but they could not seem to separate themselves. The sudden but slight shift of the boat threw him in closer to Angelique. With all his heart, he took advantage of it, and gently brushed his lips against hers. For a brief moment time stood still for the two lovers as they gazed into each other's eyes.

Then, from somewhere behind a voice cried out, "Someone is blocking the passageway. Clear the path."

The magical moment was over. Angelique Marie was pressed forward by the oncoming crowd and past Jean Paul.

She tried to keep his gaze, turning her head back to see him, but the crowd pushed on. Jean Paul staggered to get his bearings. It was a brief encounter they would remember forever, but it would not be their last.

∽

CHAPTER 22

Jean Paul wanted desperately to follow Angelique Marie, but the press of the crowd was too much. With a heavy heart he continued up the narrow passageway to the gentlemen's smoking room. Angelique was pushed into the large hall that doubled as a dance salon and searched the room all night for a glimpse of him. But her search was in vain and they were not able to meet again that evening.

Because Monsieur DuPrey's *Indiaman* was sailing in a few days, he had to leave the party early taking with him the prized beauty of the evening, his daughter, Angelique Marie. There was much to be done before they got underway.

Within the week, Jean Paul was installed as the Captain of the *Indiaman*, and enlisted nearly all of his old crew from the *Diablo*, who were thrilled by the prospect of acquiring so much treasure without a fight. They loaded the ship with the spices and supplies in a most joyful manner, singing all the old familiar pirate chantey songs.

Bateaux, the quartermaster, was asked to captain the *Diablo* with Coquelin as second-in-command. They were to follow the *Indiaman* back to Europe, effectively retracing the Portuguese navigator, Vasco da Gama's path out of the Indian

The slight shift of the boat threw him in closer to Angelique.
Jean Paul gently brushed his lips against hers.

Ocean, rounding the Cape of Good Hope, continuing to the western coast of Africa and onto Lisbon. The entire crew was excited.

They had traveled for two years and were ready to go home. Spirits were high and guards were down.

Before Jean Paul set sail, he dispatched a swift moving corvette to Madagascar with news for Captain Moulin-Bleu to hasten his recovery because he, too, would soon become a legitimate employee of the East Indian Trade Company. Captain Moulin-Bleu would be delighted. The life of a pirate was wearing thin on the old man. Soon all ships left the port of Goa India and were on their way back to Africa loaded down with valuable spices.

Monsieur DuPrey, while acknowledging Jean Paul as Captain of the *Indiaman*, kept a wary eye on him whenever his daughter was on deck. He tried in vain to keep Angelique occupied with books and such while at sea, but she was only interested in learning the workings of the ship and navigation through the waters, subjects that Jean Paul was particularly knowledgeable about.

Although Monsieur DuPrey was aware of the growing romantic interest between his daughter and Jean Paul, he should have noticed the attention that the Butcher of Paris paid to her. Neither Monsieur DuPrey nor Jean Paul recognized the increasing fixation that the Butcher had with Angelique Marie. Angelique was also oblivious to his growing fascination and completely disregarded his advances. Zuba Vachem may have shown an interest in her, but she was accustomed to men admiring her and just ignored them. Fate would have a hand in this thorny dilemma.

For the time being, however, the Butcher of Paris was not an immediate threat as he was sailing a day behind them as Captain of the *Slaver*. But his developing fondness for the daughter of Monsieur DuPrey, had quickly turned into a full blown obsession and he became intent on kidnapping her. He had nothing but time to arrange his plot to snatch up the exquisite beauty.

The African bound monsoons bore the entire fleet to the Gulf of Aden with great speed and so when the fleet reached the coast of Africa, the entire crew begged Captain Jean Paul to let them go ashore to stretch their sea legs. Jean

Paul agreed hoping, himself, to find a quiet moment alone with Angelique Marie.

The two day leave provided more free time than the crew could handle. The African coastline was not the most exciting location and after a day or so on shore, the crews relaxed and allowed sailors to freely board each other's quarters. Even Angelique became bored and decided to explore. Normally this would not be a problem as they knew each other well, but with the insidious plans of the Butcher, these liberties were ill-advised.

Angelique, furnished with her newfound nautical knowledge, began to explore the *Diablo* comparing it to her father's great ship, the *Indiaman*. She found it fascinating and asked the crew many questions about the workings of the ship. Most of the crew allowed her a respectful distance, and so she felt comfortable touring the ship unescorted. She knew quite a bit about the *Indiaman* from her conversations with Jean Paul and now she had explored all she could on the *Diablo*, so she carelessly meandered onto the *Slaver*.

Once on board the Butcher's ship, she noticed a distinct difference in attitude with the sailors, but she ignored it and became engrossed as she walked through the unused slave quarters. It was unthinkable that all those men, women and children could survive in such small, unclean lodgings.

Angelique did not pay attention to the crew slowly surrounding her until she finally felt an eeriness. She then tried to nonchalantly back away, only to find she could not escape. The men appeared on all sides of her, quickly blocking her exit. Fear set in as she tried one door and then another, until she was violently pushed into the captain's quarters.

She tried to scream, but the Butcher covered her mouth

and wrapped a piece of cloth around it. No sound could escape and her frightened eyes shifted about the cabin looking for help, somehow to escape, but none was found. All she saw in return was evil, beady, pirate eyes with toothless, foul-smelling pirate grins, smirking back at their new captive. She was now a prisoner, and she had told no one where she was going, not her father and not Jean Paul. Her only hope was that someone from the *Diablo* had noticed that she left that ship and boarded the *Slaver*. In her gut, though, she knew how naive she had been and prayed that Jean Paul would find her before it was too late.

It had turned dark and although Monsieur DuPrey had grown accustomed to his curious daughter's extended absences, she had never missed dinner before and he began to worry. Jean Paul did not know where she was either and worry set in to panic as they searched every village tent and makeshift building near the shore.

The crew of the *Diablo* and *Indiaman* joined in, even some of the crew from the *Slaver* assisted. The Butcher showed earnest concern for her whereabouts, claiming he saw her on shore walking toward the jungle.

All night long crewman with large torches walked the shoreline and into the jungle calling out her name. She could hear them, but could do nothing to let them know where she was.

Early the next morning, the *Slaver* quietly slipped away into the sea with the Butcher's precious cargo hidden, tied and gagged in his personal quarters.

The *Slaver* was nearly a day's journey ahead, before Jean Paul surmised that Angelique must be on board Zuba Vachem's *Slaver*. He questioned every sailor and pieced together what he could, until finally coming to the conclusion that the *Slaver* must have gone up the Red Sea. Jean Paul was furious, for while the *Indiaman* and the *Diablo* were commissioned to travel the Indian Ocean to Madagascar, the love of his life was headed in another direction entirely, toward Egypt. Jean Paul's anger was monumental. He had been outfoxed right under his nose.

Monsieur DuPrey was beside himself, and felt extremely guilty for not watching over Angelique more carefully. He knew the only one who could save her was Jean Paul, and so they decided to separate. The *Indiaman* would continue south to Madagascar to pick up Captain Moulin-Bleu. Bateaux would captain the ship until then. Coquelin would accompany Jean Paul on the smaller *Diablo* heading north into the Red Sea.

Before Jean Paul left, Monsieur DuPrey placed a small bag of jewels in his hand and said, "Find her! Do whatever it takes, just find her alive!!"

DuPrey placed a bag of jewels in Jean Paul's hand and said, "Find her!"

Jean Paul called his crew to arms and prepared to race the *Diablo* as fast as she would go toward Egypt and the Mediterranean. They searched day and night for the *Slaver*, but could not find her. Coquelin, then, with his keen eyes spotted the *Slaver* near the shore.

They swung the ship toward the shoreline, but they were too late. The Butcher had already abandoned his ship, ramming it into the sand, and commandeering the first caravan heading north toward Jerusalem.

Jean Paul quickly boarded the abandoned ship searching for his love, but she was nowhere to be found. He rummaged through the *Slaver* hunting for any sign of Angelique. A ripped piece of her gown was laying on the floor in the Captain's quarters. Now he knew for certain that Angelique had been there and he would do whatever it took to find her.

With nothing but the leather sack of diamonds, given to him by Monsieur DuPrey, Jean Paul followed their trail into the land of Christ. He instructed Coquelin to take the Diablo back to Madagascar and meet up with the *Indiaman* as originally planned. He would find Angelique and the Butcher of Paris or die trying.

Bateaux was now assigned the duty of bringing the *Indiaman* to Madagascar and delivering its command to Captain Moulin-Bleu with instructions to sail the vessel to St. Malo where the agents of the French East India Company would break the cargo down into smaller lots for delivery to all the spice dealers along the Mediterranean seaboard.

Even though Moulin-Bleu would command the *Indiaman* from a chair mounted on the deck, he was more than capable of commanding the boat safely to France.

Four months at sea and Moulin-Bleu would be rolling with the ship in his pegleg. Plans were to meet Jean Paul and Coquelin in France where he would be paid handsomely, a quarter of the profits from the cargo if none were damaged.

∽

Jean Paul began his search for Angelique Marie
among the Muslim shops

CHAPTER 23

The Holy Land of Jerusalem in the eighteenth century was a land of many nationalities brought together, no doubt, by the press of pilgrims toward Christ's crucifixion mount. The buying and selling of holy relics, real or fake, around the site quickly became a lively trade. Eventually, gold, silver and diamond dealers established themselves as part of the marketing mêlée there known as the Way of the Cross. After all, the steps did follow the way to the crucifixion mount where the leader of all Christianity died on a cross.

The Muslims, no particular friend to the Christians, readily recognized the monetary value from these travelers and quickly set up shops filled with supplies and relics. These Muslim shops were strategically placed at the edges of the steps ending at the top of the mount.

It was at the bottom steps, however, that Jean Paul began his search for Angelique Marie in earnest. As he climbed the steps he would inquire within each store the whereabouts of a young white woman with blue eyes and light brown hair. With his bag of diamonds, Jean Paul was prepared to pay handsomely for any hint of information that the owner would give him.

Although the Muslim traders could put a price on any

wares in their store, they were reluctant to put a price on human flesh, slave or not, especially if the ownership of the slave could not be established by the seller of the goods.

Women slaves were never violated by their owners because damaged goods, or used women, brought no premium in the marketplace. Because of this, Angelique Marie's virginity would never have been abused by the Muslims. Her high market value would have been kept intact. And Jean Paul knew that a bag of diamonds would insure her virginity as well as loosen the tongues of her would-be sellers.

Suddenly, as Jean Paul was leaving a shop on the tenth step he was violently thrown out the door and flattened onto the steps below by a horrendous explosion. The force of the blast knocked him face down into the dusty walkway and onto his stomach.

Jean Paul lost consciousness for awhile, but when it returned he spied what appeared to be a dismembered hand clawing a bag of diamonds right in front of him. In that maddening moment, he grabbed the bag and covered it up. He could not explain the dismembered hand clutching the sack, but he knew that there had been an attack and he did not plan to stick around long enough to ask why.

When his hearing returned he could make out the noise of a gathering crowd approaching and so without hesitating he hid the bag of gems under his cloak, the bloody hand still clutching the sack, and raised himself off the ground, staggering frantically to the top of the mount. There, he found an unlocked door which opened onto a community of monks walking toward him. They were absorbed in prayer.

Vaulting past them he rushed down a staircase that led to the street below and the church from where the monks had apparently come from. There in the dark shadows of the church building, Jean Paul saw a most curious sight; a Franciscan monk was poking his arm out of the church window and proceeded to drop a ring of keys to a group of Muslims below, apparently standing guard. The Franciscans were locking themselves into the church for the night with the firm belief that the Muslims would unlock the church doors the next morning, placing their safety in the hands of their Muslim brothers for the night.

Jean Paul crossed the square at the bottom of the steps and found a harness of horses waiting in a stable.

As the sun began to set, he carefully untied one of the horses and silently led it to an alley away from the church and

Jean Paul carefully untied a horse and silently led it to an alley

any bystanders. There he quickly mounted the beast and rode swiftly south toward Jericho.

When next he stopped, he watered the horse and took a closer look at the now putrid smelling hand still clutching the sack of diamonds in his pocket. He was aware now that these diamonds were not his, for he felt his own bag tied securely to his waist. The purple fingers were still gripping the bag of diamonds and he cringed as he removed each of the death-gripped digits from their stranglehold.

Angelique must have been here.

He quickly tossed the grotesque hand away and tied the bag firmly under his cloak. Then prodding the horse onward, Jean Paul disappeared into the black night.

He followed the Sea of Galilee all the way to a copse of trees whose soft shadows beckoned him to rest. He had ridden all night and into most of the morning, and so the call to sleep had become overwhelming. He tied his horse to a tree and fell fast asleep.

How long Jean Paul slept, he did not know but he was awakened by a sharp poke to his breast and on the other end of the lance was a mounted knight dressed in a white tunic with a red cross emblazoned on his left breast.

"Ho, ho, what have we here?" sounded a deep baritone voice, "Friend or foe of the Knights Templar?"

Jean Paul slid away backing up against the tree as he tried to clear his head.

"We defend the Jordan River where Christ was baptized, and although we are but a remnant from the great Knights Templar we are called to this most holy office."

Jean Paul felt the sharp lance poking his chest again.

Jean Paul was awakened by the sharp poke of a lance
from a Knights Templar.

"Now, I ask you, do you wish to venerate or desecrate
this most holy site?"

"I search for a woman, a most beautiful young woman,
a royalty of France, who was kidnapped not two weeks ago
and brought into this land. I vowed to her father that I would
find her and I intend to do that or spend my life trying. I
wished for her to be my bride, and I will not rest until she is
found," replied Jean Paul mournfully.

The Knight was visibly moved by Jean Paul's promise
and replied, "Come then fellow traveler, we will search together.
We still follow our Lord's admonition to help all Christian
travelers when they follow in the footsteps of our Lord."

Jean Paul rose to his feet, while the tall, elderly knight moved in closer and looked firmly into his eyes, "We know this country like the back of our hands. If she is still here, we will find her."

Just then three other knights appeared from nowhere and drew in closer to them as the elderly knight continued, "Most of our order has left this sandy flea-bitten desert for the Isle of Rhodes, but there is still a few of us here and we carry on our ancient pledge to help all Christians who follow the Christ."

"We need the challenge," added a smaller framed knight, who was just as robust as the other.

The band of four knights agreed in unison as one of them finally called out, "Lead the way, pilgrim."

Then all four knights turned simultaneously to the south and began riding away as Jean Paul hurried on his horse to keep up.

A month's journey of searching began.

At times, Jean Paul and the four knights would ride together in their small entourage through the cities and bazaars of Syria, Yemen, and the coastal plains surrounding the Mediterranean. At other times, they would split up to search out caves, caverns, and oasis springs that were well known to the locals as hideouts for refugees from the law. Their search was to no avail and as each day passed, the group became more convinced that Angelique Marie was no longer a prisoner of these sand dunes.

Jean Paul, too, wearied of their campaign and knew that he had exhausted their resources. He knew he must leave the honorable knights and intended to do so when they arrived in Lebanon.

The smell of the sea guided Jean Paul's steps to the dangerous Mediterranean where the Barbary pirates were active. The Barbary corsairs engaged in razzias, or raids on coastal towns to capture Christian Slaves and sell them at slave markets in Africa and Morocco.

With their blessings, the knights paid off a Turkish mercenary captain to allow Jean Paul onto his ship bound for the Isle of Rhodes. From there Jean Paul would be on his own to secure passage to the African coast, if need be. Jean Paul bid farewell to the kind knights, and asked for their prayers. The knights blessed him and began their long journey back to Jericho.

❦

Muslim Barbary pirates captured Christian women
and sold them into harems.

Turkish mercenary ship, *Kapitana.*

CHAPTER 24

Thought it was late in the year and the winter storms were battening the coast, Jean Paul took ship for the Isle of Rhodes leaving messages up and down the coast for Coquelin to follow him.

It was Jean Paul's luck that the worst storm of the century would provide the wind to his sails. The storm lasted a fortnight, disemboweling the riggings of the freighter fluyt which left them nakedly vulnerable to the wild sea. No one knew where they were bound and sea-sick as they were they could care less. They were wards of the waves until land was sighted. It mattered little if friend or foe would greet them onshore.

To his surprise, Jean Paul spotted a French tricolor flag, half blown to bits, but still fluttered in the cool evening breeze on a nearby shore. Jean Paul knew they must be nearing a small corner of France.

With admittance on the Turkish mercenary ship, *Kapitana*, Jean Paul thought he was heading to the Isle of Rhodes in Greece, but this wild storm drove the ship further away to the small southern island of Malta, just off the coast of Sicily.

The tempest had blown directly west from Egypt, and although the Mediterranean Sea was constantly plagued by local winds, this one was the Khamsin wind, a dry, dusty, hot southerly wind in Egypt. Once it hit the dry Sirocco and Ghibli southerly winds moving eastward from North Africa, a gale force squall and heavy rains tossed the ship about like a toy, causing a "following sea" that reminded him of his lost love, Angelique Marie.

Malta had been recently conquered by Napoleon, in 1798, and was now solidly French. Even though the island flew the Tricolor flag of the French Revolution, Jean Paul was grateful to have made it alive and on French soil, preferring the Revolutionaries to the unpredictable and brutal Barbary pirates.

During the months that Jean Paul lived and traveled with the knights, they had told him of a church built on the small island of Malta, called St. John's Cathedral, named after John the Baptist, patron saint of their order. So, after the ship had docked, Jean Paul felt a sudden and immediate urge to visit the church. He did not know why or how but as he moved, he felt a strange closeness to Angelique Marie. More urgently now, he scanned the island to find a church steeple, but none could be seen.

St. John's Cathedral's was built after the Great Siege and its plain facade was flanked by two large bell towers that reflected an austere military post more than a grand cathedral. But inside, the baroque artwork could rival any of the great churches of Rome. Jean Paul listened intently as he heard the two great bells of Malta began to peal, urging him on.

He entered the church.

In the early morning sunlight, Jean Paul could make out a familiar face kneeling at the communion rail.

The baroque artwork of St. John's Cathedral on the Island of Malta.

The cool, morning breeze had flushed color into her cheeks. When Angelique Marie turned to face Jean Paul, he fell to his knees in grateful thanksgiving. He had found her at last.

But, he did not notice a dark figure lurking in the shadows behind a stone pillar. It was the Butcher of Paris, who grabbed Angelique Marie's arm half dragging her to the side exit and flung her into a waiting carriage. As the carriage sped away he thought he had failed again.

Jean Paul had raced from the cathedral, untied a horse and charged after the carriage carrying Angelique Marie.

Within the hour, Coquelin's *Diablo* arrived, driven by

The Butcher of Paris grabbed Angelique Marie and
flung her into a waiting carriage.

the remnants of the same storm that Jean Paul had encountered.

"Rouse the crew and arm them and follow me," shouted
Jean Paul as he rode past Coquelin, "I've found her. Come quickly."

Jean Paul knew the road from the docks to the Cathedral
were littered with debris from the recent storm and he hoped
that it would slow the carriage down. The unpaved road was
littered with timber and fallen stones which lay haphazardly in
the road causing the carriage to shake violently from side to
side.

Jean Paul was less than fifty yards behind the coach
when the front axle snapped, careening the carriage onto its
side and spilling it occupants into a mossy sand bank which
cushioned their fall. Angelique Marie and her maids lay
unconscious in the carriage.

"Stand and deliver," screamed Jean Paul as he approached
the wreckage.

The Butcher who was leading the van on horseback,
turned his horse about and road directly toward Jean Paul. Within

seconds the woods rang with the clash of arms as the two combatants traded blows with each other.

While the Butcher's men came streaking from the docks, Coquelin and the men from the *Diablo* began to arrive. Within a quarter of a hour, the conflict between the two sides began filling the tranquil countryside with mayhem and slaughter.

Soon the makeshift battlefield was reduced to a few pockets of talented swordsmen, including Zuba Vachem, who had studied fencing at the écoles of Paris and Moscow. Most pirates were not a match for the old man with only one good hand.

Jean Paul's youth, agility and élan was a lightening flash with the rapier. He sliced through the pirates like butter. Coquelin was covering his back, armed with his voodoo lance, the very spear that had been given to Jean Paul long ago by the Benin Kinkajou tribe. Jean Paul had little to worry about from the enemies at his rear.

But as the battle continued Zuba appeared to be distancing himself from the field, intent on escaping. And so Jean Paul switched tactics and ran right toward the Butcher ignoring all the scuffles that were in his path. Coquelin ran frantically behind him. Zuba Vachem was not prepared as Jean Paul struck a blow to the Butcher's head.

But the Butcher was not easily brought down, and parried the blow with the blunt part of his blade. The maneuver, however, left his torso unguarded, and that was all that Coquelin needed.

As he caught a glimpse of the uncovered torso, he whirled about thrusting his spear deep into the heart of the Butcher.

Du Gu Do….Du Gu Do….Du Gu Do!!! yelled Coquelin.

"I ONLY KILL ACCOMPLICES TO EVIL."

The Butcher immediately dropped to the ground. The eight foot long mahogany lance swayed back and forth in his lifeless body as if to ensure that its target was dead, and the engraved words appeared to darken as life left the Butcher's body.

Suddenly, all of the Butcher's men froze in place and looked at the lifeless body. They, then, threw down their weapons and immediately quit fighting.

Jean Paul took advantage of the pause, and quickly ran to the carriage where he found Angelique slowly waking up. He held her in his arms and repeated her name over and over, hoping that she was not injured. She finally awoke, smiled weakly and touched his face.

Jean Paul held her in a long embrace, kissing her forehead and checks over and over until he finally kissed her lips.

"I will never let you go again."

᱐

CHAPTER 25

It is here, dear reader, that the French manuscript ends and as all good readers know the rumors begin. Jean Paul and Angelique Marie were married in St. Malta with Coquelin as their best man.

From there, they sailed to America in the Spring of 1800, making their way to Carondelet, Missouri, a small town south of St. Louis, where they lived with a friend, Henri Chatillon until the birth of their first child.

Coquelin would not leave Jean Paul for love nor money and so he traveled with them to the New World.

Angelique's sister, Claire, also joined them for the journey to America and found a home with the Sisters of St. Joseph of Carondelet where she taught Native American Indians.

Monsieur and Madam DuPrey sailed for America in 1801 after he had secured the fur trading rights west of the Kaw River in the Kansas Territory.

Captain Moulin-Bleu took over the captaincy of the *Indiaman* until 1804 when it sank in a violent hurricane off the coast of Jamaica. No word was heard from the old pirate until he turned up in Cape Hatteras in the Carolinas.

He was running an Inn for wayward seamen.

Jean Paul and Angelique Marie were married in
St. John's Cathedral on the Isle of Malta.

His signature pegleg was posted on the sign in front of
his establishment and all who knew him, found his stories
outrageous and unbelievable. Though, no one really believed
the stories, they found them quite compelling. He was content
with that.

The Quartermaster, Charles Bateaux, continued sailing
for the French East Indian Company, eventually retiring in
1830, never to have seen the Americas.

The diamonds? The ones that travelled the world in
Jean Paul's pockets. They are reported to be resting comfortably
in a niche in a wall of the Cathedral of St. Louis, hidden in a
leather bag behind a stone.

To this day, up the 10th step, near the south wall of the
Cathedral one can see a repaired stone mortar. It is there that
Jean Paul, grateful for his life and for the love of his life, in the
silence of the night, chipped away at a stone, removed it, and

placed a small leather bag deep into its groove.

Then he covered it again with well-mortared stone. Carpenters never found it, priests never looked.

Cathedral of Saint Louis

Why did Jean Paul not spend the diamonds? In Carondelet, Missouri you ask? In a remote countryside village in the middle of the New World? Someone owning diamonds surely would be suspect of having lived a dangerous youth. Maybe of even having been a pirate!

Ainsi-soit-il

ى